Do swans fly?

"Go for it, Lauren," said Cindi.

I raised my right hand and then I took off. I pumped my arms. I felt confident, like a champion athlete who couldn't miss. I went through it all in my mind, imagining myself flying through the air, hitting the springboard, and flying over the vault like a swan in flight.

Do swans fly?

I hit the springboard and aimed with both feet for the blue takeoff line on the board. The only bird I resembled was the dodo or the penguin.

Patrick tried to catch me and shovel me onto the vault, but my feet slipped and I kicked him.

"Oww!" said Patrick. "Are you trying to kill me?"

**Other Apple paperbacks you
will enjoy:**

The Little Gymnast
by Sheila Haigh

Sixth Grade Can Really Kill You
by Barthe DeClements

Mitzi Meyer, Fearless Warrior Queen
by Marilyn Singer

Oh Honestly, Angela!
by Nancy K. Robinson

The Friendship Pact
by Susan Beth Pfeffer

The Baby-sitters Club #2
Claudia and the Phantom Phone Calls
by Ann M. Martin

THE GYMNASTS

#1 THE BEGINNERS

Elizabeth Levy

AN
APPLE
PAPERBACK

SCHOLASTIC INC.
New York Toronto London Auckland Sydney

ISBN 0-590-44050-0

12 11 10 9 8 7 6 5 4 3   3/9

Printed in the U.S.A.   28

To Ria Assante and the McBurney Team:
Althea, Angie, Carla, Cat, Mara, Sarah, and
Vanessa

Life-Styles of the Limber

"I can't believe I let you talk me into this," I moaned to Cindi, my best friend. "I already feel sick to my stomach. Fear can make you carsick. It's a proven fact, maybe not scientific, but it's proven. I'm the proof."

"Don't be sick in my car," said Cindi's brother Tim with a laugh. Tim was driving us to gymnastics class. Maybe it was his driving. He'd just got his license. But I didn't think his driving was that bad. Tim was in that brief stage that all of Cindi's older brothers had gone through when they were willing to drive us anywhere.

I clutched my stomach. I like to see Tim squirm.

Cindi laughed, but I wasn't exactly joking. I was on my way to my first gymnastics class in a long time and I wanted to go back home, maybe back to bed.

Cindi and I took gymnastics classes when we were little. Some adults laugh when kids talk about something we did when we were younger. They think it's so cute. But I'm eleven now, and I quit gymnastics three years ago when I was eight. I would have been perfectly happy to live the rest of my life without ever falling off a balance beam again, but Cindi wasn't.

Recently a new gymnastics academy opened near us, the Evergreen Gymnastics Academy, which advertises itself as "shaping the future . . . beginners through elite." Well, I wasn't exactly a beginner, and I sure wasn't elite. "Academy" made me think of lots of little miniature cadets acting like windup toys, flipping in the air. But Cindi got it into her head that our entire friendship depended on me going back to gymnastics with her.

I really felt scared. I'm always scared when I do something new. I'm not chicken. I do it anyway, but I'm scared, at least a little.

"This is going to be so great," said Cindi. "Mom checked out the new coach, Patrick. He's young. He just graduated from the University of Colorado a couple of years ago, but he was already coaching at a club in downtown Denver. He's

2

cute. And he's looking for girls with experience. That's us."

"That's you. I can't remember any of the moves." Then I giggled. "Well, maybe some of them. Remember the time I was showing off on the vault and I slipped, landed on my head, and did a perfect headstand by mistake?"

"Yup," said Cindi. "You claimed it was your Yogi Bear move. Don't you remember how much fun we used to have?" she pleaded. "You've got to give it a second chance. You've got the perfect body type for it."

That's a polite way of saying I'm short. Short is good in gymnastics. But I'm not exactly skinny. I'm not fat, mind you, but I did hear my uncle once say that I was built like a fireplug. I didn't take it as a compliment. I have straight black hair that I wear in a short pixie cut with little pointy bangs that are supposed to be a bit punk according to the guy who cuts my hair. I don't look punk. At my best I can go for cute, an eleven-year-old short pixie who happens to be shaped like a fire hydrant.

Cindi and I are like Mutt and Jeff. Cindi is having her second growth spurt. She's about five inches taller than me, and would like to stop growing. She's worried she'll turn into a giant. We have often talked about making a trade. I'll take a couple of her inches, and she'll take a couple of my good grades. Getting good grades has always been easy for me; growing hasn't.

Cindi's whole family is athletic. She has four older brothers. Cindi is not just the baby of the family, she's the only girl. Cindi wants to be a gymnast because it's the one sport no one else in her family does. Cindi says that coming from a big family makes you want to stand out.

I wouldn't know about that. I'm an only child. I do know that I love Cindi and her family. There's always a lot of laughing going on at her house.

Cindi's so enthusiastic about everything that it's easy for her to talk anyone into anything. Including talking me into going back to gymnastics.

When I quit gymnastics in the third grade, it was because I was secretly afraid I wasn't good enough. My parents let me quit. They thought it wasn't my thing. Besides, they thought it was taking up too much time. I didn't fight them when they suggested I had better things to do with my life than hanging from rings.

Part of me was really excited about trying it again. Maybe I would turn out to be better than I thought. Maybe I'd be really good.

But as we got closer to the academy I got more and more nervous. Tim pulled into an alleyway

4

behind the Evergreen Mall. "Where is this place?" I asked.

"Keep going," said Cindi. We drove past the public part of the mall down a road that had nothing around it except a few cottonwood trees by a dried-up stream.

"I was right," I groaned. "This is the end of the world. I'm going to be abandoned here, endlessly trying to swing from a stupid bar. Maybe I can sue my parents for letting me take gymnastics again. Maybe I can sue you."

"You know what, Lauren?" asked Tim. "You haven't even imagined the worst part."

"What's that?"

"You could like it," said Tim. "You could love it."

Cindi laughed. "Yeah, she'll probably love it. But will she tell us?"

I laughed, too. "I promise. If I love it, I'll let you know."

"Yeah," said Cindi. "You know Lauren. She'll be great at it, and she'll love it, but she won't tell me because I was the one who talked her into it."

"Cindi, you've got to understand that some people are not meant to live life upside down."

"It's a proven fact," said Cindi and Tim in unison.

Who needs brothers and sisters when you have the Jockett family? I laughed. "Well, it could be fun to do it again," I admitted. "I wasn't that bad at it."

"And this time we've got a chance to make a real team," said Cindi. "That's the whole point of this place. We may get to be on a team. We'll compete. We'll go around to meets. We may even travel around the state."

"What if you make it, and I don't? No . . . I'm sorry I said that. I'll love watching you from the sidelines. No, I won't. If you make the team, I want to be on it," I babbled.

"You will," said Cindi. "I think Patrick puts everyone on some sort of a team."

"I wonder what the uniforms look like. What am I talking about? I hate competition."

"That's a lie," said Cindi. "You get good grades. And you had that grin on your face when you beat Matt Davis in math."

"I know," I admitted. "But it's not sports."

"Lauren, don't knock it till you try it," said Tim. "Sports are great."

"They're great for the Jockett family, because all of you are jocks. Maybe I could join a couch potato competition."

"You're no couch potato," said Cindi.

"I know. But maybe I could become one."

"Give it a chance," said Tim. "I can just see

6

you and Cindi at the Olympics, 'up close and personal.' TV reporters will come and interview me. I'll tell them the first time I drove you and my sister to gymnastics class, you almost got sick in my car. Then I dropped you off and you came back a star."

"I'll say, 'Yes, I owe it all to my best friend Cindi and her brother Tim.' It's an amazing story, ladies and gentlemen. Two girls, one short, one tall. Friends since kindergarten — "

"Which one wins the gold?" asked Cindi.

"We stand on that little step together. It's a tie. The first tie in Olympic history. Of course, you almost push me off the step because by the time we're in the Olympics you're six feet tall. The world's tallest gymnast."

"And you're the world's fastest talking gymnast," said Cindi.

"Right," said Tim. "The little gymnast who wouldn't shut up."

Just then a maroon Corvette tore down the dirt road and passed Tim going about sixty miles an hour.

"That's one cool car," said Tim, putting his foot on the gas pedal and trying, unsuccessfully, to catch up.

The maroon Corvette pulled to a stop behind a huge gray warehouse with high windows around the side.

Above the door swung a small sign that said "Evergreen Gymnastics Academy," with silhouettes of kids doing gymnastic tricks off the branches of the evergreen tree. There was nothing else around. The warehouse was just a gray cement cube that looked like one of those out-of-the-way places that the TV detectives are always going to alone to meet the villains.

"This is where the elite meet and greet?" I asked.

"You've got fast company if that kid works out here," said Tim. A black girl got out of the passenger side of the Corvette. She was wearing a leather bomber jacket with a white bunny rabbit fur collar, and a jeans miniskirt and cowboy boots.

"Maybe I will take some classes after all," said Tim.

"Stick to football," said Cindi.

"You sure you don't want me to go in?" said Tim.

"No," said Cindi. "No way. And you don't have to pick us up. Lauren's mom is doing that."

I looked up at the Evergreen Academy sign. It sure didn't look like much of an academy. It didn't look like a school of any sort. My mom works for the Denver Board of Education, and my dad's a high school principal, so even more than most kids, I've been around schools all my life. In a way, it's weird because my mom is like my teachers' boss, and they're always a little bit afraid of her. It sounds cool but it isn't. One thing about gymnastics, I wouldn't get any special treatment because of my mom's job.

This gymnastics school wasn't what I pictured. Even the sign was a little funky. I liked that.

We watched as the elegant black girl opened the door to the warehouse.

Then I opened the car door. I took Cindi's hand. "Why do I feel like I'm six years old and starting my first day of school?"

Cindi giggled. "Remember when we started first grade and I wet my pants and you were the only one who didn't tease me?" she asked.

"That's 'cause I was scared, too," I said. "Just like I am now."

"I am, too," whispered Cindi.

Then we both laughed together. If we were both scared, how bad could it be?

"Come on," I said, suddenly feeling a little brave. "Let's go check out the life-styles of the limber."

Up Close, Personal, and Scared

The black girl was really very beautiful. She had high cheekbones, and she was wearing purple lipstick. It was a color most people would only wear on Halloween, but on her it looked good.

I had a good chance to study what she looked like because she was standing right in the middle of the entranceway, making it impossible to get around her.

"Excuse me," I said. "Can we get in, too?"

The girl jumped. "Sorry," she said. "How long were you standing there?" She was wearing braces on her teeth and when she talked she didn't look quite as old.

"We just got here, too," I said. "It's okay. No big deal."

"Easy for you to say," said the girl.

I wondered what her problem was. I looked around her shoulder into the gym. Maybe she was as scared as I was.

The warehouse was huge and light drifted in from the skylights above, giving it an eerie otherworldly look.

Most of the floor was lined with blue mats, some two inches thick, some as thick as mattresses. Some mats were piled high into hills, others were shaped like triangles and octagons. It looked like a soft Lego game for giants and the giant kids had forgotten to clean up.

Rings hung from the ceiling. At one end of a runway of mats was a regular vaulting horse, and at the other was a soft trapezoid horse that came apart in three breaks. At the far end of the gym were a set of parallel bars, and the uneven parallel bars for girls. In another area there was a very low beam almost two inches from the floor, and then another low beam about a foot off the floor, and then a high beam almost four feet off the floor. This area looked like Goldilocks' playroom: one beam too low, one beam too high, and one beam just right. I had a feeling that the baby beam would be my style.

The gym was already full of a group of about twenty-five little kids, some only four years old, boys and girls divided into small groups. One group was hopping across the mats like kangaroos.

Another group of five little kids was perched on the balance beam like a bunch of little starlings. Another group just seemed to be lying down on the mats.

In between the younger kids, a few older girls who looked like they were in junior high were stretching out. The young kids all ignored us, but the older ones looked at us curiously.

A curly-haired man with big biceps came over to us. He was dressed in an Evergreen T-shirt with the club logo on it.

He *was* cute. I guessed he was the coach. He gave me his hand. It was full of calluses. "I'm Patrick Harmon."

"I'm Lauren, Mr. Harmon," I said. "I haven't done gymnastics in a long time. I mean, we're talking years, sir."

Coach Harmon laughed as if I had said something funny. "Cindi said that her best friend would be coming. She said that you used to take gymnastics and that you were great, but that you'd say you were lousy."

"Was I right, or was I right?" said Cindi.

"You described her perfectly," said Coach Harmon.

"Except I'm really not very good, sir."

"You can call me Patrick. I don't believe in formality with my kids. You'll want to call me a lot of other names by the time we're through. Just think of me as your average friendly benevolent dictator whom you can call by his first name."

He laughed, but I wasn't sure he was joking.

"Did Cindi really tell you I was good?" I said.

Cindi nodded.

"Today we'll do a little testing," said Patrick. "See where you are, if you like it here, and *if* you fit into our program. I don't take everybody, you know." He winked at me, but he looked pretty serious.

Now I really was scared. I had been so worried about *not* liking it that I hadn't thought to worry about whether or not they would want me.

"Lauren was good when we were little," said Cindi.

"We'll see," said Patrick.

He turned to the other girl. "Darlene, I'm so glad that you made up your mind to work with us. And I'm glad you've met Cindi and Lauren."

"We haven't exactly met," I said. "Hi, I'm Lauren Baca. This is Cindi Jockett."

For some reason Darlene looked uncomforta-

13

ble. "Hi, I'm Darlene Broderick," she mumbled.

"Darlene, your dad came to see me, and he signed the form, so you're all set for three months. We're thrilled to have you working with us."

Darlene fidgeted. She looked even more nervous than me.

"You girls are going to be my pinecones," said Patrick. "That's the name I give to my newcomers."

"Nuts," I whispered.

Darlene giggled.

Luckily Patrick didn't hear me. "I'm always excited when we get girls your age who've had a little gymnastic training. I'm putting together a team, and we could use some new blood. I want to see what you can do."

"I can't do much," I said quickly.

"Just change in the locker room and let me be the judge of that," said Patrick.

"What did you get me into?" I hissed at Cindi. "He takes this stuff really seriously. All this talk about his team."

"That's why it's so neat he moved out here. He's supposed to be one of the best."

The dressing rooms were much nicer than I expected, with wall-to-wall carpeting, a shower room, and lockers with combination locks built in.

Cindi and Darlene each got a combination because they had signed up for a series. I had to use a long locker at the end of the room, and Patrick gave me a lock to use for just one day. Maybe I should have just gone whole hog and talked my parents into letting me sign up for the whole shebang rather than just one class.

Darlene put on a stretch lycra pink leotard and tights with glitter in them. It shimmered in the harsh overhead lights.

"That's beautiful," said Cindi. She giggled. "Personally I go for the more casual look." Cindi just pulled off her jacket and announced she was ready. She was wearing an extra-large Bronco T-shirt that practically covered her baggy beige gym shorts. She stuck a barrette in her hair to keep it out of her face.

"Wait till you see mine," I said. I had a brand-new leotard that my grandmother bought me on sale. Grandma's always finding things on sale. She's a great shopper. I loved the leotard; it was pink with gold and green butterflies on the front. We're not talking little delicate butterflies; we're talking about giant flying insects parading across my chest. Anyone can have sweet butterflies. I thought giant green and gold butterflies showed style. At least that's what I thought at home. However, now as I looked at myself in the mirror I decided there was probably a good reason why the store had three dozen of them on sale.

I crossed my arms in front of me and walked across the locker room to where Cindi was talking to Darlene.

"How long have you been doing gymnastics?" Cindi asked Darlene.

Darlene looked at herself in the mirror. She ran her fingers through her hair, pulling it over her right eye. Her hair was much longer on the right side than the left. It sure was a weird haircut, but sort of sophisticated.

"I think I hate my hair," said Darlene. "I'm sorry, what did you say?"

Cindi giggled. I could tell she was nervous. "I asked if you did a lot of gymnastics and you answered 'I hate my hair!' "

Darlene laughed nervously, too. It was good to know we were all nervous. "Sorry. Yeah, I've been taking gymnastics since I was seven."

"How old are you now?" I asked. "Fifteen?"

Darlene laughed. "Twelve," she answered. She had dark purple nail polish on her fingers and on her toes.

"Twelve!" I exclaimed. "You look so much older."

Darlene nodded her head. Suddenly she looked shy. "It's a drag being tall."

"I know what you mean," said Cindi.

"Everybody always thinks I'm older just because I'm tall," said Darlene. "And it makes gymnastics harder."

16

"Finally," I said. "An advantage to being short."

"It is in gymnastics," Darlene said seriously. Cindi nodded.

Actually I didn't think people thought Darlene was older just because she was tall. Purple nail polish didn't make her look young. I mean, Cindi's tall, but she doesn't look like a teenager.

"What grade are you in?" I asked.

"Seventh," said Darlene.

"We're in fifth," I said.

"What school do you go to?" asked Cindi.

It was almost as if we were cross-examining her.

"St. Agnes," Darlene said.

Cindi and I looked at each other. St. Agnes was the most snotty of the private schools. We'd never met anybody who went there.

Then Darlene surprised me. "I hate St. Agnes," she said. "I'm glad to be meeting some new kids. It's a drag when people think they know everything about you."

As we walked back out to the gymnasium, I whispered to Cindi, "I think that means we're not supposed to ask her any more questions."

"There's something mysterious about her," said Cindi. "I wonder how good she is."

I looked at Darlene. She just looked like she knew what she was doing. "I think she's gonna be good."

17

"So do I," said Cindi.

When we got out to the gym, a girl in a leotard with a video camera started filming us.

"What are you doing?" I asked.

"I'm taking 'before' and 'after' pictures," she said with a giggle.

Cindi and I stared at her. I could feel myself blushing.

"But we haven't done anything yet," I said.

"I know," said the girl. "But I like to see what the new kids are like. Just forget that I'm here."

"That's not exactly easy when you've got a camera in my face," Cindi said.

"Introducing Cindi, Lauren, and Darlene," I said into the camera. "Up close, personal, and scared."

The girl laughed. But I wasn't really kidding. I was scared.

3

Testing! Testing!

Patrick was waiting for us out in the gym. "You girls warm up. Then we'll put you through some tests."

He must have caught my grimace at the word "tests."

"The tests are just for me," he said. "So I can see what skills you've got and how strong you are. Nothing to worry about."

"Nothing to worry about?" I asked. "That's like what the vampire told itself when it was being tested in school."

"What kind of test does a vampire take in school?" Patrick asked.

I liked him. He was a perfect straight man.

"A blood test," I said.

Darlene laughed out loud. I could make her laugh. I liked that in a friend.

Cindi scrunched up her lips, something she always does when she's nervous. I giggled. That's what I do when I'm nervous. Giggle and make bad jokes. But at least Patrick seemed to like bad jokes.

"All right, girls," Patrick said. "We want you to have fun. Lauren, you can tell all the jokes you want, but you still have to work."

"Fun?" asked Darlene. "You want us to have *fun*, and you're going to *test* us?"

Patrick laughed. "It's not school, Darlene. You can't fail my tests."

"I bet *I* can," I said.

Patrick shook his head. "I'm going to have Becky warm you up. Most of you will probably end up in Becky's group also. She competes in the class IV A. It's the highest level we have going now. Every day I pick one of you to lead the warm-ups. It builds leadership qualities." He called out into the middle of the floor for Becky to come, pronto.

Becky sauntered over, her rib cage held high like a dancer. She was the one who had been videotaping us earlier. She was petite and pretty, and she put us through our warm-ups like a drill sergeant.

It began easily enough. We started by gently

20

walking around the gym on our toes. Unfortunately that lasted all of about two minutes. Becky told us to start running on our toes, and then she commanded us to skip.

"Stop!" she yelled sharply. Cindi stopped short and pushed into me, and I pushed into Darlene. "You all skip like elephants," yelled Becky. "Raise those knees. Okay, come over here on the mats. Now circle your arms. Circle your hips. Pretend you've got a Hula-Hoop around you."

I wasn't sure how good a gymnast Becky was, but she was certainly good at giving orders. I tried to follow her, but her hips moved like they were on ball bearings, and I knew mine were going up and down like a seesaw.

"Hey, you, with the pink leotard on!" Both Darlene and I stopped, but it was soon clear who she had in mind.

"You with the baby leotard. What are those? Flying cockroaches? Is that your insignia from your last club?"

"They're butterflies," I managed to gasp out.

"Well, they look like they're being attacked by killer moths. Keep your rib cage tight. You're just supposed to move your hips. Hold the rest of your body still."

"I'm trying," I croaked. I glanced over at Cindi, who seemed to be doing the circling motion perfectly.

21

"Okay, down on the mats," said Becky. "Stretch in a pike position."

I looked around. I couldn't remember a pike position from a flounder.

Darlene sat on the floor with her legs straight in front of her. Then she took hold of her toes and pulled her head straight down to her knees.

I tried it. There were about two inches between my knees and my head. I wished I had longer hair so that at least it would look like I was closer.

"Okay," said Becky in an impossibly cheery voice. "Let's do some stomach crunches."

"It sounds like a breakfast cereal," I said.

Darlene laughed. Cindi lay on her back with her knees in the air and her ankles crossed. Apparently stomach crunches were a form of half-sit-ups devised by a torture expert. We were supposed to do thirty.

I flopped back onto the mat after fifteen.

"What are you doing?" Becky demanded.

"I'm doing the beached whale position," I said. "I'm very good at it."

"Yeah, well, you have the baby fat for it," said Becky.

Cindi stopped doing her crunches. "Hey, you can't talk to Lauren like that," she said. I liked that she was standing up for me.

"That's not baby fat . . . that's muscle," I grunted.

Becky laughed at me. "We'll see. You kids haven't even been tested yet."

"I'd like to test her I.Q.," whispered Darlene.

Cindi and I both laughed.

"Okay," said Becky. "You kids are having so much fun we'll work on splits." Apparently working on splits meant that I tried to do a split while Becky sat on my back. I hollered that it hurt.

Luckily Patrick heard me. "Careful with her, Becky," he shouted from across the room where he was helping a girl on the uneven bars. "She's the one we don't know anything about."

That made me feel great. The unknown quantity. I wanted to show them. Unfortunately I wasn't sure I could. Somehow I'd find a way.

Patrick came over to us and put his arm around Becky. "Good job," he said.

"They're a little slow," said Becky. "Especially the little one in pink."

"I'd like to challenge her to a spelling bee," I whispered to Cindi and Darlene.

"That was a hard warm-up," said Darlene. "You haven't had much gymnastics, have you?"

"I wish I had kept it up," I said. "And I never had lessons at a place where they took it so seriously."

"It gets better," said Darlene.

"All right, girls," said Patrick. "Come with me. Now we have the fun part."

I think this will give you a good idea of Patrick's true nature. He really did think that this was the "fun" part. He walked us over to a cement wall that had a big tape measure pasted to it like in the nurse's office at school.

He had each of us stand next to the wall and stretch up our arms to the highest point. Naturally, as the shortest one with short arms, my reach was the lowest.

"Okay, girls, go chalk up," said Patrick.

At least I knew what that meant. Even at our low-key gymnastics classes, we used to chalk up. Ground-up chalk is how you know you're doing gymnastics. Gymnasts use it on their hands to make sure they get a good grip on the bars. Sometimes it seems like gymnasts don't do anything, except maybe go to the bathroom, without first chalking up.

Chalking up was one of my favorite activities when I used to take classes. It isn't scary and it isn't work. It's a little like getting a chance to play in the mud.

Cindi and Darlene walked confidently over to a plastic container that looked like a giant eggshell with a hole in it. Inside lay a mound of chalk dust. Cindi and Darlene each stuck their hands in the chalk, clapped their hands once to get the loose dust off their palms, and walked back over to the wall.

24

I stuck my hands into the white dust, clapped my hands once, and got chalk all over my pink leotard. I sneezed, and got chalk on my nose. Then I nervously wiped my hands on my thighs and got white dust all over my tights.

Patrick looked at me strangely. "I think I just flunked chalking up," I said.

Patrick shook his head. He wasn't laughing at my jokes anymore.

By the time I got back to the wall, Darlene was swinging her arm forward and jumping as high as she could, leaving a white chalk mark at the peak of her jump. She got up over a foot higher than her first mark.

Cindi jumped next and left a white mark a little below Darlene's.

Then it was my turn. "I don't understand what I'm supposed to do," I said.

"Just jump as high as you can and leave a mark at the top," Patrick said.

I jumped as high as I could and my white smudge was about six inches under Cindi's.

"Great!" boomed Patrick. I looked at him. I hated to be patronized.

Then he took us over to the rings. "I want to see your leg lifts. I want to see how strong you are in the stomach. Don't use your shoulders. Do as many as you can in ten seconds. Lauren, you can go first this time."

I figured that having short legs might be an advantage for leg lifts. I hung from the rings. Patrick took a piece of foam about a foot long and put it between my feet.

"See if you can do it without dropping the piece of foam."

I didn't lift my legs once before the foam came floating out from my ankles, dropping to the ground like a leaf. Darlene giggled.

"Let me try again," I said.

Patrick shook his head. "Try it without the foam." I immediately felt like I had been demoted. After three leg lifts I thought my arms were coming out of their sockets, and my stomach ached. I practically fell onto the mat below the rings.

"Good," said Patrick, but Cindi did seven perfect leg lifts without dropping the foam once, and Darlene did eight.

"Okay," said Patrick, still sounding cheery. "Now we'll have an old-fashioned race. In gymnastics it's not how long you can run that we're worried about, but how fast you are out of the blocks. I'm looking for your explosive power."

"Explosive power!" I exclaimed. "If I want explosive power I'll join the army."

"If I take you, you'll feel like you *have* joined the army," said Patrick.

I swallowed hard. That was a big "if."

The starting line was a huge yellow crash mat

giving us something to push off against. Patrick stood twenty yards away with a stopwatch in his hands.

"Okay, go!" he shouted.

Darlene had the longest legs but she was the slowest. Cindi and I were a half step ahead of her right from the beginning. Cindi and I have always raced together. I pumped my arms as hard as I could. Cindi got ahead. I felt as if my lungs were bursting, but I kept pumping, and at the very last minute, I dove for the finish line the way I've seen them do at track meets on TV.

I won!

Cindi rolled on the mat next to me.

"Great race," she whispered. And then I had a horrible thought: Had Cindi let me win just so I'd look good and make the team?

Can You Flunk Creative Rest?

I was still out of breath from our race when a woman dressed in a leotard and shorts brought another girl to our group.

"I'm sorry we're late," said the woman.

"I was wondering where you were," said Patrick.

"At the last minute, my daughter decided to try it," said the woman with a sigh. "Jodi, this is Coach Harmon."

"Call me Patrick. It's nice to meet you, Jodi. It's a real thrill for us that your mom moved here from St. Louis. Girls, this is Sarah Sutton and her daughter Jodi. Sarah will be one of our coaches. She was on our national team when she used to compete, and she had her own gymnastics school in St. Louis. We're lucky to have her. Jodi, your mom says that you're lukewarm about gymnastics." Patrick winked at me. "That's okay. You can keep Lauren company. She's not so sure herself."

Jodi stood with her weight on one leg, not even looking at us. She had long blonde hair that she wore twisted in a neat braid, and she had knotted friendship bracelets on both wrists and her ankles. The friendship bracelets looked worn, as if they were about to fall off. She didn't smile at Cindi, Darlene, or me; instead she looked around the gym as if she were bored.

"Your mom must be really good," said Darlene.

Jodi shrugged. "Mom didn't want me to come, but I figured what the — "

"Jodi," said her mother sharply. "That's not true, Patrick . . . that I didn't want her to come. I'm glad Jodi's decided to keep up with her gymnastics."

"I was just testing the three new girls," said Patrick. "Jodi, you can do the tests you missed later with your mother. Right now, I'd like to see you on the uneven bars."

I rolled my eyes again. "Uh, Patrick, we didn't even have uneven bars at the place where I used to go. Maybe I should skip this one."

"Not a chance, Lauren," said Patrick, picking me up before I knew what was happening. "You're not quitting on me yet." He hoisted me over his shoulder like a sack of potatoes. I couldn't help giggling. "You let me do the teaching . . . I think you've got real potential."

Potential is one of my least favorite words. I hear it and I want to run for the hills. Even though I get good grades, my teachers are always saying to my parents, "Lauren is not working up to her potential."

Everyone has seen the uneven bars on TV. The high bar is set about seven feet above the ground, the low bar about five feet, and the object is to swing from both, sometimes hitting the low bar with your stomach. You don't want to look like a monkey, but rather like a dancer with pointed toes who just happens to be swinging at great speed, bouncing from bar to bar with perfect grace.

Patrick told me to chalk up. No one even goes near the uneven bars without chalking up. Then he lifted me onto the high bar, a mere seven and a half feet above the mats. "Don't be scared," said Patrick. "I just want you to hang there for a second and get the feel of it." I was left like the poster of the kitten who's hanging on to a broomstick for dear life. The caption says, "Get a grip on yourself."

My arms felt like they were going to come right

out of my shoulders. My grip was slipping.

"Good," said Patrick. "You're nice and straight. You're doing great." He let go of my legs. "Now try a pull-up. Don't be scared, I'm right here. Just pull your chin over the bar."

"Easy for you to say," I said. I tried to pull myself up. I got my nose over the bar. My arms were feeling like spaghetti. I hung back down again.

"Good," said Patrick. "Do it again. One more time for me." I struggled to pull myself up. This time I only got my eyes over the bar, before I had to hang back down. I almost fell, but Patrick caught me, and I got a firmer grip on the bar.

"Just for the fun of it, we'll try a pullover," said Patrick. "It's like a somersault, only you're holding onto the bar."

"Fun?" I grunted.

Patrick laughed. "Straighten out your arms and hold yourself away from the bar," he said. He helped me push my body at a forty-five-degree angle away from the bar. "That's what we call a cast," said Patrick. "It will give you the momentum for your swings and circles. It's important to learn to do it right."

"That's because if you don't, you'll end up in a body cast!" shouted Jodi.

"Great," I grunted.

Then before I knew quite what I was doing, I swung away from the bar, and Patrick caught me around the other side. I had done a somersault around the high bar! To tell the truth, it was sort of thrilling.

"Wonderful," said Patrick. "You can let go." He gently lowered me to the ground.

I half crawled to the mat on the side of the uneven bars and sat cross-legged next to Cindi. I looked up. I couldn't believe what I had just done. I think Cindi was amazed, too.

"Okay, Jodi, let's see what you can do."

Jodi chalked up and then grasped the lower bar. She swung so her toes almost hit the high bar; she pulled herself up by circling around the bar, released the low bar, and the momentum of her turn pulled her up as she let go of the low bar and jumped to the high bar. She was flying!

"Hey," said Patrick. "I wasn't in position to spot you. What are you doing?"

"Sorry," said Jodi, as she hung from the high bar and did one back pullover after another until I was dizzy watching her. Then she spread her legs wide onto the low bar and circled it like a windmill. Finally she jumped off.

Darlene and Cindi applauded. Patrick and Jodi's mother frowned.

"Next time, I'd appreciate it if you gave me some

warning of what you're going to do so I can spot you. That could have been dangerous," said Patrick.

"Sure," said Jodi, out of breath. "But I thought you said you wanted to see what I could do."

"You showed me a little bit more than I bargained for," said Patrick.

Jodi sank down next to me. "You were terrific," I said.

Jodi shrugged. "I like the bars."

"I wish I could do that," said Cindi.

"I've got a secret," whispered Jodi.

"What's that?" Cindi asked.

"I don't care about falling. I just like to fly," said Jodi. Then she laughed. Cindi and I looked at each other. Gymnastics sure attracted some strange characters.

Darlene was next. Darlene wasn't as good as Jodi. She could only do three pullovers from the high bar.

Then it was Cindi's turn. I knew Cindi wanted to do well. She started off great. She did a perfect back hip pullover and then rested on her thighs on the high bar for a second. She pushed herself up. "Great," said Jodi's mother. "Now do another one."

Cindi tried, but as she was circling up, she couldn't pull over; her knee caught on the lower bar and she hung upside down like a hanger in a jumbled closet.

"Good try," said Jodi's mother as she helped her down.

Cindi looked a little discouraged.

"Okay, let's go to the beam," said Patrick.

"I wish he didn't sound so enthusiastic," I mumbled. The balance beam is just four inches wide. You're expected to do all the things you do on the floor, cartwheels and somersaults, leaps and jumps, all on a board that's no wider than your average half-chewed pencil.

"Always look for the end of the beam," whispered Darlene. "It's easy."

"Easy!" I exclaimed. Darlene went first. No wonder she said it was easy. On the beam her body just looked right. Her stomach was pulled in, her chest high, her hands graceful. She looked like a wonderful ballerina who happened to be on a tightrope. She could make her body move in waves. She leapt across the beam like a cat. Then she was balancing on one foot and leaning into a forward roll; that's a somersault on a little four-inch board, five feet above the ground.

"Let me see a roundoff dismount," said Patrick.

Darlene started a perfect cartwheel at the end of the beam, her hands landing inches from the end. Her feet came together and twisted her body around, and she landed with her hands high in a V facing the beam, just like all the gymnasts you see on TV.

Cindi and I stared at her in awe.

Then it was Cindi's turn. Cindi tried to show off and do a running mount onto the beam, but she overshot and landed on the other side of the beam. She fell onto the mats on her shoulder.

"Good fall," said Patrick.

Cindi's cheeks were red.

"Try a straddle mount," said Patrick.

Cindi was breathing hard by the time she stood up, and her legs were shaking. Patrick stepped closer to the beam so that he could spot her if she fell again. She jumped onto the beam and stretched her legs into a split. Then she curled her toes and stood up.

Cindi did a tuck jump, tucking her feet underneath her and keeping her arms wide open. She almost lost her balance again, but she caught herself.

"Good," said Patrick. "Very good. Let me see a straddle dismount."

Cindi jumped off the beam opening her legs wide, but she had too much force and she ended up falling forward.

"That was good, Cindi," said Coach Harmon. "You've got courage."

Cindi's cheeks were two bright spots of red. She stole glances at Darlene, who had been so good.

I took my turn on the beam. I used to like the beam. It isn't as scary as it looks. I did a leap and that was fine. But then I tried a simple forward somersault on the beam, and before I knew it I was under the beam on the mats.

"Are you okay?" Patrick asked.

I nodded. I started to get back on the beam.

"Thanks, Lauren," he said. "That'll be all." I figured he had seen enough.

Then Patrick asked us all to climb on the beam and stand facing him.

"Me, too?" I asked.

"You, too. This is something even our beginners do."

When we were all turned the right way, Patrick said, "Stand on one foot." I tried, and unbelievably I didn't fall off.

"Now close your eyes," said Patrick as he took out a stopwatch.

"You've got to be kidding," I said.

Patrick shook his head. I had a feeling he was beginning to find me not so amusing.

I closed my eyes and I heard someone laughing in front of us. I peeked through my half-closed eyelids. It was Becky, and she had her stupid video camera on us. She was standing with two of her friends.

I fell off the beam. I landed with such a thud that Cindi, Darlene, and Jodi opened their eyes and fell off, too. We started laughing. Patrick frowned and went over to the end of the beam and stood with Jodi's mother. He kept looking at his clipboard and then back at us and frowning.

"What are you doing with that stupid camera?" I asked. "You made me fall."

"You made yourself fall," said Becky. "That's one thing you've got to learn in gymnastics. If you fall, it's your fault. We just wanted to check out the competition. So far, I don't think we have anyone who can help."

"Help?" I asked.

"We compete as a team," said Becky. "And Coach Harmon's team came in second last year. We need some new girls. I was on the team. Second is pretty good. It's not last, but it's not first."

"Yeah," said Becky's friend. "Patrick told us his new place would attract a lot of new girls. He's really looking for some kids who can help us, but I don't see anyone here."

"You're wrong," I said. "You should have seen Jodi on the uneven bars, and Darlene is terrific. So's Cindi," I added quickly, feeling disloyal.

"Yeah, well, none of you can hold your balance," said Becky.

"Okay," said Patrick, coming back to us. "I think I've seen enough."

"I bet he has," whispered Becky.

"Excuse me, Becky," said Patrick. "I want to talk to the new girls alone for a second. Why don't you do some handstand push-ups? I want to see your upper body strong. I don't need you sitting around here."

Patrick put one arm around me and one around Cindi and guided us all to a corner of the gym. We sat in a semicircle on a mat around him.

"I think this group has a lot of potential," he said. "I'm excited about working with you. We have a good team that I think you can be a part of, but in the beginning, I'd like you to try to work together as a unit. You've got too much experience to just be pinecones. In a few weeks, we'll see where you fit with our regular team, but I don't want to push you into competition outside of the club too early."

I raised my hand. "Excuse me," I said. "I don't think I really belong here, Coach Harmon, I mean, Cindi's been to gymnastics camp this summer, and Jodi's mom's a coach." I turned to Jodi. "You've probably been doing it since you were two, right? And Darlene . . . well, you can take one look at her and tell she's as flexible as a cat.

I mean, when we were doing our splits, no one should be able to get in that position, but I've never done this . . . and. . . ."

Patrick interrupted my babbling. "Are you through?" he asked.

"Well, I'm just trying to be honest," I said.

"Come with me, Lauren," said Patrick. I figured he wanted to take me aside to tell me privately that I was right. He didn't want to work with me.

Patrick walked me over to the wall with the tape measure. "Look at your chalk mark, Lauren," said Patrick.

"It's the lowest," I admitted. "It's like I was telling you, I don't belong here."

Patrick shook his head. "No, it was the best. You've got power. You jumped eighteen inches over your height. That's fantastic. Besides, I liked the way you went about the tests. I can tell a lot about a girl. You didn't give up when you couldn't keep the foam between your feet. You were scared on the high bar, but that didn't stop you from trying. You've got a lot of potential. Sure, you don't have the skills yet of the others, but Lauren, I'd be glad to have you on my team."

I felt myself blushing. Patrick walked me back over to the others. "What do you say?" Patrick asked, sticking out his hand.

I grinned. I took his hand. "Just call me a pinecone," I said. "Out of little pinecones grow big ice cream cones, or something like that."

Patrick smiled. "You'll see. By the end of the month, you'll be in competition."

"Uh, excuse me?" I said. I felt this was all going a little too fast.

"That's right," said Patrick. "I want to get you used to competition. In one month, we'll put on a pinecone exhibition, but it'll just be for the club. It'll be a show for your parents and other guests. It's how I always start off my girls. It gives you a goal. In just one month, you'll be competing in an in-club meet, but we'll have real judges, and we'll see what you're made of."

"I don't know if I'll be ready for that in one month," I said.

Patrick put his arm around me. "Don't worry. I have a hunch about you, Lauren. I think you're going to surprise everybody. Now, listen up. It's time for the best part. It's what I call 'creative rest.' I want you to lie down on the mats. Bend your knees and cross your arms over your chest. Now close your eyes. Imagine yourself up on the beam. But the beam is as wide as the floor. Every move you make is perfect."

My eyes were closed. I imagined the beam spreading out from its sides like peanut butter. Then I imagined a layer of mayonnaise on top of the peanut butter that made the beam so slippery that I gushed around like an ice skater out of control. Peanut butter and mayonnaise is one of my favorite sandwiches, and suddenly I realized I was starving. But I think if Patrick could have read my mind, he'd have told me that I'd just flunked creative rest.

5

Dust-Bunnies From Outer Space

We walked to the dressing room, and for the first time I noticed the little things that were already sore. My hands hurt, the back of my legs felt like rubber bands stretched too far. This was only ten minutes after class; I could imagine how I'd feel the next day.

"Your mom was really at the Worlds?" Cindi asked Jodi. "That's incredible."

Jodi stopped biting her fingernails. "You should see my sister," said Jodi. "She's on the Air Force Academy team."

"You must be like one of those circus families," said Darlene. "It must be hereditary."

"What do you mean?" Jodi demanded.

"Nothing," said Darlene. "I meant it as a compliment. You didn't have to snap my head off."

"Sorry," mumbled Jodi. "It's just that every time I go to a gymnastics class . . . never mind."

"What's wrong?" I asked.

Jodi started biting her fingernails again. She shrugged her shoulders. "Oh, nothing. . . ."

"Hey, maybe we'll all end up in a circus act," said Cindi. Trust Cindi. If there was an awkward moment she'd always try to make it better. "We'll be a circus act called 'The Perilous Pinecones,' " she said. "This will be a historic moment. 'They met on a sunny, fall day in Denver, Colorado. Four girls, nondescript.' "

"Who are you calling nondescript?" asked Darlene.

"Well, you're right. Nobody would call you nondescript," admitted Cindi.

I liked the idea that somehow this moment would go down in history. The four of us would find fame and fortune. I continued Cindi's rap. Cindi and I were always starting stories and letting the other one finish. "There was one girl, short, who had tried to quit gymnastics, but her best friend dragged her by the hair. . . ."

"I didn't drag you," protested Cindi.

"Besides, she doesn't have much hair to drag," added Darlene.

"Let me finish," I said. "But the short one turned out to be a. . . ."

"Somersault freak," said Darlene, giggling.

"Lauren? She gets dizzy if she does one somersault," said Cindi.

"That's mean," I said. "I haven't gotten sick once, yet."

"Thanks for small favors," said Darlene. "I wouldn't want to be under you on the uneven bars when you upchuck."

"Oh, gross," said Cindi. "Don't even put it in her head. She'll do it."

Jodi listened to us giggling, but I realized that she felt left out.

"Then there was the fourth star," I said. "She came from the Flying Flippers, world-famous gymnasts, but Jodi had a secret. . . ."

Jodi giggled.

"She didn't care. The gymnast who didn't care! It made her dangerous."

"What do you mean, 'dangerous'?" Jodi asked.

"I meant it as a compliment," I said.

"It must be great to come from a family of gymnasts," said Cindi.

"It's got its ups and downs," said Jodi. She had made a joke!

"I only come 'cause I get free classes. But maybe I won't. If you guys don't want me."

"You're good," said Cindi quickly. "You're the best one of the four of us."

Darlene looked like she wanted to protest.

Jodi shrugged, but she looked pleased that Cindi thought she was good. Darlene and I looked at each other. It was strange how we had been together just an hour, and it felt like we were linked together like a real team.

Darlene opened the door to the dressing room. Becky Dyson and several of her friends were waiting for us.

"It's the new rookies," said Becky. "We always like to look over the pinecones lying on the ground. I saw you on the bars," Becky said to Jodi. "You were pretty amazing. Sorry I didn't get it on film."

"What's with you and the videotaping?" I asked.

"It's a wonderful tool," said Becky. "Patrick can't afford one yet, but Mom and Dad let me bring mine so I can videotape my moves and study them."

"Jodi's mom was at the World Championships," blurted out Cindi, thinking it was something to be proud of.

Becky waved her hand up and down as if that news was just too cool to fathom.

"We know," said Gloria. "She's going to be our coach."

"We have a tradition at the Evergreen Club," said another one of Becky's friends. "We like to find out which of you kids is the strongest."

We all looked at each other. "Probably Darlene," said Jodi. "She looks like the strongest to me."

Darlene looked angry, although for the life of me I couldn't figure out why. I thought Darlene would have been proud of being strong.

"Not me," said Darlene to Jodi. "I'm sure you're the strongest. You've been doing gymnastics the longest."

"Little Lauren is pretty strong," said Jodi.

"Little Lauren?" Cindi exclaimed.

"Yeah, whose side are you on, Jodi?" I said.

"Sorry," said Jodi. "I meant it as a compliment. You are strong."

"Little Lauren," I said to myself in disgust.

"Enough," said Becky. "I bet I'm stronger than all four of you put together. I'm not that much taller than Lauren, but I'm stronger than all of you."

The four of us looked at each other. "You? You're a tiny little thing," said Darlene.

Becky looked smug.

"She's mighty strong," said one of her friends.

"Well, I hate to brag," said Becky with a smile, "but I *can* lift all four of these tiny pinecones at once."

Although Becky was strong-looking, she didn't look *that* strong. "You've got to be kidding," said Cindi. "Nobody's that strong."

Becky just smiled. "I can lift all of you at once," she said. "There's a certain technique about it."

"Bull," said Cindi. "Not even Beef Broderick is that strong." Beef Broderick was a lineman for the Denver Broncos and according to the papers there was nobody bigger or tougher than Big Beef Broderick.

"If Becky says she can do it, you've got to believe her," said another of Becky's friends.

"I've seen Big Beef Broderick," I said. "Nobody's stronger than he."

"Where did you see him?" demanded Becky. "Denver Bronco tickets are impossible to get."

"Oh, I've seen him," I said with a smile. Actually I had only seen him on television doing commercials. I didn't even watch football, except at Cindi's house. My parents had to be the only ones in the entire metropolitan area who didn't care about the Broncos. But I wanted to get the conversation away from who was the strongest in the room.

I hadn't been to any football games, but I did know when I'd met a bully. There was a lot of bully in Becky.

"I don't see what he's got to do with this," snapped Darlene.

I wished that Darlene had kept quiet. If we could have got them arguing about who had or hadn't seen some dumb football game, Becky might have forgotten her scheme.

Becky smiled. She seemed to sense that she was back in control.

"Beef Broderick doesn't have anything to do with this. It's just that I'm stronger than he is."

Cindi giggled.

"You find that funny?" Becky asked.

Cindi nodded. "Look, all my brothers are football players, and any one of them is stronger than you are, much less as strong as Big Beef Broderick. I don't care how long you've been doing gymnastics or how many push-up handstands you can do."

"Do you think your brother or Beef Broderick could lift all four of you pinecones with *one* hand the way I can?" asked Becky.

"You can't do that," I said.

"I can lift four of you at once," said Becky. "It's all in the technique."

"I bet you can't," said Cindi, putting her hands on her hips and jutting out her lower lip.

Becky reached up and patted Cindi on the head. "You've got yourself a bet, conehead."

"Who are you calling a conehead?"

"That's Coach's name for you rookies, isn't it?"

"When he calls us pinecones, it sounds nice," said Cindi.

"Isn't that too sweet for words?" said Becky.

"Yeah, Patrick thinks we're so good, all four of us will probably be competing for him in a month," said Cindi.

"Oh, yeah?" said Becky. "All four of you are going to make the team! Patrick would never put four losers on our team."

"You wait and see," said Cindi. "Patrick is very happy to have us. He's so excited that he's going to put on a special meet for us."

Becky started to laugh. "You're so dumb. He just has that meet for the newcomers so the weenies will drop out. I bet none of you are here in a month."

"I'll take that bet," said Cindi.

Becky laughed. "Okay, and if I win, you have to lift four of us. But don't you want to see me do it?"

"I bet Patrick's the only one who can lift four at once," said Cindi.

Becky turned to her friend Gloria. "Isn't that cute? I think this little pinecone has a crush on Patrick already."

"I do not," snapped Cindi.

"Besides, what's wrong with having a crush on Patrick?" I asked.

Becky laughed at me. "I bet you have a crush on him, too," she said.

"So what," I answered. "I think *you* have a crush on him and you're just jealous because he likes us."

"Oh, little Lauren . . . she's got a great big crush on Patrick," teased Becky. "He'll drop you faster than a speeding bullet."

"A speeding bullet doesn't drop," I said. "When it drops, it's not speeding anymore."

"It's a proven fact," said Cindi and I in unison.

"Yeah, well, Patrick will drop you 'cause you're no good," said Becky.

"That's up to him, not you," I said, my hands on my hips.

"Yeah, he'll drop you as fast as I'll lift you up."

"You can't even lift one of us," I argued.

"Lauren," said Darlene, shaking her head. "Anyone can lift you up, no problem."

"Well, maybe she can lift one of us," I said. "But she sure can't lift all of us. Let's see this stunt."

"It's all in the technique," said Becky. "You've got to line up just right. The whole trick is to keep you level."

"Watch and you might learn something, pinecone," said Gloria. "This is a fantastic trick. It's been done at the Christmas show."

"Oh, yeah," said another of Becky's friends. "But then it's got real snow. It's beautiful."

"Snow?" asked Jodi.

"She's just talking about the glitter we all use

50

for the Christmas show. That's got nothing to do with this trick," said Becky. "Now I need you all lying down on the floor."

"You're going to lift all four of us from the floor?" asked Darlene. "That's impossible, even for Beef Broderick," she added in a whisper.

"This I want to see," said Cindi. She lay down on her back on the floor.

"Now the rest of you, lie right down next to her, close together, like peas in a pod," ordered Becky.

I hesitated a second and then I lay down beside Cindi and Darlene lay down next to me. Jodi leaned against a locker.

"What about you?" I asked.

"Count me out," said Jodi. "I'll watch you lift the three of them."

"It's much more dramatic with four," said Becky.

Jodi shook her head.

"Come on," I said. "We're a team."

Jodi hesitated. "Oh, all right. But something tells me this is a mistake."

Jodi lay on the floor next to Darlene. "What do you do, scoop us up with a giant shovel?" she asked.

"No," said Becky. "I'll pick you up with my bare hands. The only way I can do it is if you lock your arms and legs together."

We all linked our arms at the elbows.

"Twist your legs together. Darlene, you put one leg over Lauren, and now Cindi." By the time Becky had finished ordering us about we were crisscrossed on the floor like pretzels.

When we were completely pinned against the floor, Becky said, "Now close your eyes. I don't want you getting dizzy on me when I lift you up."

"Ready, get set, go," said Becky.

I had my eyes closed tight. Unfortunately my mouth was open. Suddenly it was full of chalk.

Becky and her friend dumped the entire contents of the plastic egg all over us. I started coughing and tried to get up, but my left leg was under Darlene and she couldn't stand up. By the time we got untangled, we looked like doughboy quadruplets.

Becky and her friends laughed so hard they could hardly talk. "You know what we call rookies?" sputtered Becky. "Not pinecones, that's just Patrick's word. We call rookies like you worms, and worms eat dirt. Worms, kids. You guys are worms. Welcome to the Evergreen Academy, worms."

Becky and her friends took their towels and went to the showers.

Darlene was the first to get up. She looked at herself in the mirror. "Well, I always wanted to see what I looked like white," she said.

That cracked me up. I stood next to Darlene and looked at myself in the mirror.

"I look like a dust-bunny from outer space," I said. Cindi laughed so hard at that she fell back down into the chalk dust.

Darlene started laughing, too. "Dust-bunnies from outer space, that's what we are . . . that's our name for ourselves."

Cindi stood up, scattering white chalk dust all over the locker room. "We'll get her back," she said. "The dust-bunnies' revenge."

"Should we go tell Patrick what they did to us?" Darlene asked.

Cindi shook her head, spreading white dust all over.

"No," she said quickly. "We dust-bunnies from outer space fight our own battles. I'm sure Becky's expecting us to run to Patrick. We have to do the unexpected."

"What's that?" I asked.

Cindi scrunched up her face. "I don't know. But we'll think of something."

53

The Wink

By the time we got to the showers, Becky and her friends had used up all the hot water.

"Why don't you come to our house?" I said. "We can swim and plot our revenge."

"You've got a pool?" asked Jodi.

"It's not exactly my pool. I live in the Hunter Creek Town Houses," I explained. "They've got a great big pool for everyone who lives there."

Cindi put on her jeans. "Great idea. Dust-bunnies from outer space should stick together."

I tried to wipe some of the chalk dust off my arms. Since my arms were sweaty it stuck and was beginning to cake. "If we don't get into water soon, I think this stuff is gonna harden."

Darlene hesitated. "Uh . . . I'm not sure I can come over."

"Oh, come on," said Cindi. "Just for a little while. My brother will drive you home afterward. He'll drive anybody anywhere. Where do you live?"

"Uh . . . he doesn't have to drive me home," said Darlene. "Don't worry. I can have someone pick me up. But wait a minute and I'll make a phone call."

Jodi was biting her nails.

"I guess I'll be going," said Jodi.

"Hey, aren't you coming over for a swim?" I asked.

"Am I invited?" Jodi asked.

"Of course," I said. "I didn't know you needed a formal invitation."

Mom was waiting for us when we got out. She was talking to Patrick and Sarah, Jodi's mother. Mom's mouth dropped open when she saw me. "What happened to you? You look like a jelly doughnut."

"Uh, nothing," I said quickly. "I just got a little too much chalk dust on me."

Patrick looked at us curiously. "Becky told me that there was some sort of an accident in the locker room, that one of you spilled the dust. Those chalk eggs are not to be played with."

"It was an accident, all right," I said, spitting out a little of the dust that was still on my lips.

"Mom, can everyone come over to our house for a swim?"

Mom ignored me and talked to Patrick. "What is this dust?" she asked. "Lauren is allergic to many things. It's not dangerous, is it?"

"Wait a minute, Mom," I argued. "It's chalk dust. If I were allergic to that, I'd be allergic to you and Dad."

Mom didn't think that was very amusing. But it did strike me as kind of funny that here Mom was standing in a gym where we swung from bars seven feet off the ground, and she was worried about me being allergic to the chalk. Give me a break.

Patrick gave me a dirty look. I didn't think he liked me talking back to my mom. I probably shouldn't have done it in front of him. It's just that sometimes I can't resist teasing her.

"I'm sorry, Ma," I said. "But gymnastics was really, really fun. I want to keep coming. Can you sign me up now?"

Patrick smiled at me. "Lauren has a lot of potential," he said.

I was glad that he used the P word. It was one of Mom's favorites.

Mom gave Patrick a tight smile, but Patrick just gave her a wide grin back. "She's got guts," said Patrick. "We look for kids with guts."

Patrick caught me laughing. "What are you laughing at, munchkin?" he asked.

I giggled. Patrick just made me giggle. I mean, he didn't know who he was dealing with. Mom was used to my teachers telling her how nice and polite I was, and what a good worker. I don't ever remember a report card saying that I had guts. I liked the sound of it.

"Lauren and her dad and I will have to talk some more about it," said Mom. "We only let Lauren come try out because her best friend Cindi was going."

Cindi looked a little embarrassed, but nothing compared to what I was feeling.

"Mom, Patrick doesn't have to know my life history. I really, really want to join Patrick's club," I said.

"I heard you, Lauren," said Mom with a smile. She put her arm around Cindi. "I hope you're not doing it just because of Cindi. You two always want to be together." She turned to Patrick. "These two have been giggling together since they were in nursery school."

"Giggle, giggle," I said, poking Cindi in the ribs.

"Nobody sticks with gymnastics just because their friends like it," said Patrick. "That's why I love teaching gymnastics. I only get kids who want to be here. I've got a feeling Lauren's going to want to be here for herself, right, Lauren?"

I nodded my head yes. I meant it. I did want to be there.

I introduced Mom to Jodi and Darlene and finally we got out of there. Mom grilled Jodi and Darlene on how much gymnastics experience they had and how much gymnastics cut into their schoolwork.

Mom and Dad had been pretty easygoing when I first said I wanted to try gymnastics again, but I wasn't sure how they'd take it if I wanted to do it seriously.

When we got to our house, Mom made us all shower before we went out to the pool so we wouldn't get chalk dust in the water.

As soon as we got there, clouds came over. It had been hot in the morning, but September weather in Denver can be crazy. Sometimes we have snow in September, and I'm not talking about a few flakes; we've even had a few days when school closed in September because of snow. On the other hand, it can be boiling the way it had been so far this fall. Our weather changes in an instant. It can be hot in the morning and freezing in the afternoon.

The four of us were the only ones at the pool. We didn't swim long. Soon we were wrapped in towels on the chaise longues, looking like mummies.

Darlene looked up at the sky. "We used to live in Miami," she said. "That was great. I hate the cold."

"When did you move here?" Cindi asked.

"Last year," Darlene mumbled. "I dropped out of gymnastics for a couple of months. I'm really rusty."

"A couple of months!" I exclaimed. "Look at me. I dropped out for a couple of years. Maybe I'll become famous as the pinecone who dropped the farthest. Or the nut who cracked," I added.

"Yeah, but in a couple of weeks, it'll all come back," said Cindi. "You should never have quit."

"Why did you?" Darlene asked.

"I don't know. I thought I wasn't any good. And some of the stuff we did scared me."

"Did you know," asked Jodi, "that babies are born with only two fears?"

"What does that have to do with gymnastics?" asked Cindi.

"We're born afraid of loud noises and afraid of falling," said Jodi. "I think that's why kids who take gymnastics are a little weird. We're not afraid of falling."

"You're out of your gourd," said Darlene. "I'm afraid of falling. I just like feeling strong."

I giggled. "Think you'll ever be as strong as Becky?" I said. "Boy, did we all fall for that."

"I almost didn't," bragged Jodi. "I knew something was up."

"She's gonna be a pain," said Cindi. "What happened to Dust-bunnies' Revenge? We've got to think of something."

"We will," I said.

"You know, it's really, really freezing here," said Darlene, shivering.

"What season is it when you're on a trampoline?" I asked.

"Springtime," shouted Cindi, who knows all my jokes.

"Why does a tightrope walker always carry his bankbook?" I shouted.

"I don't know," said Darlene.

"In order to check his balance!" shouted Cindi. I had been making up gymnastics riddles all week and trying them out on her.

"Great," said Jodi. "We can suffocate Becky in bad jokes."

"Meanwhile, I'm freezing to death," said Darlene.

It was really getting cold by the pool, and we went back inside without coming up with a plan to get back at Becky. But we had time. We would be together almost every day after school.

"Would you girls like to stay for supper?" asked

Mom when we were dressed. "We're having barbecue. We've got plenty."

"I can't," said Darlene quickly. "My parents are expecting me."

"They're welcome to join us," said Mom. "It's just hot dogs and hamburgers."

"Uh . . . they're vegetarian," Darlene blurted out. "Look, I've got to be getting home."

"Me, too," said Jodi.

"I can't stay, either," said Cindi. "Grandma's coming for dinner. Jodi or Darlene, do you want a ride? Tim's picking me up in fifteen minutes."

Darlene shook her head. "No, I told my dad I'd meet him at the Hunter Creek Mall. I can walk there."

"Can't he meet you here?" I asked.

"No . . . it's all set," Darlene insisted.

Later that night I really wished that the other pinecones had stayed for supper. I could have used their help. My problems started innocently. Dad was cooking the hamburgers and I was helping him.

"So, how did it go today?" he asked.

"I've got potential," I said.

Dad laughed. He knows how much I hate it when teachers tell him that.

"Actually, I really liked the coach," I said. "His name's Patrick, and I guess I'm stronger than I think. I could jump real high."

61

" 'Real high.' Watch your grammar," said Dad. I hate it when he corrects me, but I guess occasionally I don't speak right.

"They don't score you on grammar in gymnastics, Dad. Anyhow, I'm not as good as Cindi or these other two new girls, but it was fun. I'm going to do it."

Dad flipped the hamburgers. I could tell he was only half listening.

"Fine," he said.

"Great. 'Cause I was worried you might think it's too much."

"Don't be silly, Lauren. I want you to do what you want."

"It'll mean I'll go four days a week after school," I said.

When Dad found out that I wanted to go to Patrick's four afternoons a week, he almost dropped the hamburger between the slats of the grill.

"That's out of the question," he said.

"Wait a minute. You can't just say that."

Dad gave me his 'look.' It's the look I've seen him give high school kids who are in trouble. He doesn't use it on me too much. Thank goodness. I hate that look. It means that he thinks he's one hundred percent right.

"Lauren, it's too much. Four days a week. You'll

be exhausted. You won't have time for your schoolwork."

"Dad, that's so unfair. My grades — that's all you talk about. How about what I want? If it were something at school that was taking four days of my time, you'd be all for it. If I joined the chess club or Spanish club or something dumb like that."

"I wouldn't call those activities 'dumb.' "

"That's not what I meant," I argued.

"You aren't even athletic," said Dad.

"That's not true. I may have explosive power."

Dad looked at me. We were both angry. Finally he backed off a little. "Explosive power?" he smiled.

"Yeah, that's what Patrick says."

"And that's good?" Dad asked.

I nodded.

Dad carried the hamburgers back into the terrace of our town house. He plunked the hamburgers down on the table. "Emily!" he shouted to my mom. "Did you know Lauren has a scheme where she's going to gymnastics every day of the week?"

"It's only four days, not every day," I said. "You have to go that often. It's the only way to learn, Patrick says."

" 'Patrick says,' " mimicked my father. "Patrick is not the boss around here."

"Neither are you," I said angrily.

"Lauren, watch your mouth," warned Mom. "Carl, I met Patrick. He's very good with the girls."

I gave Mom a look of relief.

"You want Lauren to become a gymnastics junkie?" asked my father.

"Dad," I argued. "Some parents would love it that I want to do gymnastics four times a week. It's better than just watching TV all afternoon, or hanging out at the mall."

"Neither of which you've ever done," commented my father. "I'm just worried about it interfering with your schoolwork. Down the line, you may regret it. Your grades will start to suffer and then who knows what college you'll get into?"

"I'm only in fifth grade, for heaven's sake. I don't think I have to worry yet about college."

"Lauren's got a point," said Mom, again surprising me. Usually it's Mom who's always talking about the importance of good grades. "Lauren's only been to gymnastics once. Let her try it for a while."

I quickly looked up. That's when I saw it. The wink.

Sometimes I get so mad at my parents. I knew what that wink meant. They thought I'd never stick it out. I had quit once. They were betting that I would quit again.

7

Can't Is a
Four-Letter Word

All the other pinecones had been doing vaulting from the very first week. While Patrick worked with my friends, I had to work alone with Jodi's mom "mastering" the fundamentals.

Jodi's mom, Sarah, was a great one for taking apart each gymnastics move and analyzing it.

She had me jump up and down on the springboard, the horse right in front of me, but she didn't want me to do a vault.

"Not yet," Sarah said.

"Those are Mom's favorite words," Jodi whispered to me. "Not yet."

Sarah gave Jodi an exasperated look. "Just kidding, Mom," said Jodi.

"Jodi, you worry about yourself," said Sarah. "I'll worry about Lauren."

Jodi tried her vault. She barreled down the mats, jumped onto the springboard with both feet; her hands went on the top of the horse so she was doing a handstand, but then she arched over, she lost it, and landed hard on her back on the crash mat.

Sarah ran to her.

"I'm okay, Mom," said Jodi, getting to her feet.

"You're not getting enough lift from the springboard," said Sarah.

Jodi bit her fingernail.

"Your mom's right," said Patrick.

Sarah demonstrated the correct way to hit the springboard while Jodi and I watched.

Jodi's mom hit the springboard perfectly, sailed high into the air, did a perfect handstand onto the vault, flipped over, and landed lightly on her toes.

"She makes it look easy, doesn't she?" I said.

"Yeah," said Jodi.

Sarah came back to me. "Sorry, Lauren." She smiled. "You'll be doing that soon," she said.

Jodi still looked a little shaken from her fall. "You sure I want to do that?" I asked.

Sarah nodded. "I think you've got the makings of a great vaulter," she said.

"I'll never know unless I try, I guess," I admitted. "Why don't I do one now? I'm getting sick of these baby steps."

Sarah shook her head. "You and my daughter are two of a kind. You always want to take things to the limit," she said. She smiled at Jodi. "I meant that as a compliment."

"Okay, Mom," said Jodi. "I get the point."

"Patrick," Sarah shouted. "I think it's time for Lauren to try to put all the pieces together."

Finally I was getting to try a real vault. Sarah stood on one side of the vault to catch me if I fell. Patrick stood on the other side. I felt like a pitcher on opening day who was seeing double. I had two catchers! Patrick's knees were bent, ready to take my weight.

For the past three weeks while everyone else was doing real vaults, I had been practicing with Sarah and the little kids. I spent one entire day jumping on the springboard. I had hopped onto mats. I had practiced jumping off the horse from a squat position, but I hadn't put all the pieces together. Now it was my turn!

"Go for it, Lauren," said Cindi.

"Lauren, are you going to wait all day?" shouted Patrick from the end of the runway. "Try it."

I raised my right hand and then I took off. I pumped my arms. I felt confident, like a champion athlete who couldn't miss. I figured all those days of creative rest were finally paying off. I went through it all in my mind, imagining myself flying through the air, hitting the springboard, and flying over the vault like a swan in flight.

Do swans fly?

I hit the springboard and aimed with both feet for the blue takeoff line on the board. I forgot to swing my arms behind me. I went inches into the air. The only bird I resembled was the dodo or the penguin.

Patrick tried to catch me and shovel me onto the vault, but my feet slipped and I kicked him.

"Oww!" said Patrick. "Are you trying to kill me?" He put me back down on the floor next to the springboard.

"Do you know what you did wrong?" he asked.

I nodded.

"Tell me," said Patrick, looking me in the eyes.

I looked down at the ground. I was lying. I didn't have the faintest idea why I didn't go in the air.

Patrick didn't get mad at me. "You forgot to use your arms. It's the swing that gives you momentum. Go back and do it again."

"I told you, Patrick," said Becky, who had stopped to watch. "That's one pinecone you should have left in the pod." Becky had her video camera in her hand.

"Pinecones don't grow in pods, pea brain," shouted Cindi to Becky.

68

"Cindi, mind your own business," said Patrick.

Personally, I thought she *was* minding her own business, sticking up for me. I liked it.

"Patrick, watch me," demanded Becky. She handed her video camera to one of her friends whispering, "Film me."

I expected Patrick to yell at Becky, for interrupting us. But instead he stood with his hands on his hips, studying her movements. Becky did a series of perfect roundoffs down the same mats that I was using for my run for the vault.

"That's very good," said Patrick. "But your legs are coming together late on the roundoff."

Becky nodded. "Practice on the other mats," said Patrick.

"I need you to spot me," demanded Becky.

"Sarah, you work with her," said Patrick. "I'll continue working with Lauren and the other pinecones."

"She's not strong enough to hold me," said Becky. "I need you."

I wanted Patrick to tell her to bug off, that he was working with me, but he didn't. He and Sarah watched Becky one more time. Finally, after I had thoroughly lost my concentration, Patrick came back to me.

"Okay, Lauren, are you ready?"

I was ready. I pounded down the runway and

jumped on the springboard. I felt Patrick's hand punch my rib cage as he tried to get me on the vault. My toes slipped over the edge of the leather, and I ended up bashing my shin against it.

"Ouch!" I rubbed my shin where I had fallen.

Becky laughed.

I looked at the horse. It looked so incredibly easy when the others were doing it.

I wasn't trying to do one of Mary Lou Retton's maneuvers. All I was supposed to do was get from the springboard to a squatting position on the horse and then jump off.

We weren't talking handstands or roundoffs. I had been practicing those on the mats for three weeks, but Patrick said I wasn't ready for them yet.

"Your timing is all wrong," said Patrick. He took my hand and led me down the runway.

"Let's count the steps."

"I'm not sure she can count," said Becky.

"I'm gonna count to ten, and then I'm going to clobber you," said Cindi. "Get off her back."

"I'm offering creative criticism," said Becky. "I'm trying to help."

Cindi snickered.

Becky stopped what she was doing and sat down next to Jodi and Darlene. She whispered something to Darlene.

Great, just what I needed, a whispering audience.

Patrick told me to practice taking a giant step onto the springboard.

"Take a shorter run-off," he ordered.

I was considering a long run-off. A run off the mat into the dressing room and out of there.

For about the thousandth time since we had begun, I wondered what I was doing there when everyone else knew what they were doing.

And yet, day after day . . . I kept coming back. I hadn't run off.

"Fine," I muttered. "A shorter run-off. . . ." I knew it wouldn't help.

"I've got an idea," said Becky. "Why don't I help Lauren spot the landing?"

"Landing?" I hadn't even made it to the top of the horse yet for the beginning.

On TV if you watch reruns of *Bonanza* or other westerns, guys are always taking a running start, putting both hands on the rump of a horse and vaulting into the saddle.

Believe me, if I were the Lone Ranger and someone needed help, they'd be in big trouble before I got there.

Getting onto a horse from a running start is not as easy as it looks, and the horse I was trying to get on was half the size of a real horse. It was more like trying to jump onto a Shetland pony and missing.

"Becky, you can help Lauren," said Patrick. "Stand at the end of the crash mat so Lauren can aim for you. Lauren, when you go for your landing, reach with your toes, stretch yourself out; that's how you'll keep your balance."

"Ready, aim, fire!" shouted Cindi to encourage me.

Becky stood on the far side of the vault with her video camera up to her eye.

I didn't make it.

My leg hurt, my shoulder hurt, and my stomach hurt. I lay on the mat trying to catch my breath.

"Do you know what you did wrong this time?" Patrick asked.

I wanted to kill him. In these last few weeks of gymnastics, I had found something that I hated even more than the word 'potential.' It was Patrick asking me, "Do you know what you did wrong?"

Of course I knew. I hadn't gotten over the stupid horse. Gymnastics was hard enough, and then whenever I fell there was Patrick asking, "Do you know what you did wrong?"

"I think I made a wrong turn when I decided to come back to gymnastics," I said.

I was only kidding, but Patrick didn't laugh.

It didn't seem fair to me. If I hurt myself I want to get sympathy, not a failing grade. Vaulting was scary stuff. Everything I did on the vault happened so quickly. The uneven bars look frightening, but to me the vault was the really scary one. There's no time to think. "I hate vaulting," I said. "I'll never get it. I can't."

"Lauren, you know that 'can't' is a four-letter word that we don't use here," said Patrick. "Go sit down. Jodi, it's your turn."

It was not a good day for vaulting. Jodi was trying dive rolls. That is where you literally dive over the vault and land on the mat headfirst, rolling into a somersault.

She crashed coming down and landed on her butt.

Everyone was crashing. Cindi hit the board wrong and landed on her shoulder even though Patrick tried to catch her as she slipped over the vault.

"My head!" she cried.

"You hit your shoulder," said Patrick.

"Yeah, but it's my head that hurts," said Cindi, standing up shakily.

"Your head should hurt," said Patrick. "It wasn't working. You went off the board all wrong. You were way over to the side. That's the way you can really hurt yourself."

Cindi nodded. "Does it really hurt?" asked Pat-

73

rick, playfully rubbing Cindi on the head, something he hadn't done for me in a long time.

Cindi shrugged. "Go lie down next to Lauren for a second," said Patrick. "Okay, Darlene, try it again."

Cindi came and lay down next to me. "You okay?" she asked.

"If that were a real horse, I'd shoot it," I said. "On second thought, maybe they should shoot me to put me out of my misery."

I watched Darlene try the dive roll. This was definitely a day of disasters. She fell back on her arm, and again Patrick told her what she had done wrong.

"Come on over and join the walking wounded," I said.

Darlene crashed down on our mat. Vaulting is hard for her because she's growing so fast. She's getting tall, and she can't seem to tuck her body in quick enough.

"Vaulting scares me," said Darlene.

"You?" I was surprised. It was hard to think of Darlene as being scared of anything. Darlene was a strange one. I liked her. But I can't say I felt as if I knew her at all. We almost never saw her outside of gymnastics class. After that one time she came swimming at my house, she had never been back.

"I thought it was only me, the beginner, who hated vaulting."

"You know what your problem is?" Darlene said. "You worry too much about being the beginner. You make it into this big thing: The Beginner. Well, you've been doing it for weeks now, and I get tired of hearing about The Beginner."

"Well, excuse me," I said. "Excuse me for breathing."

"I just get sick of it," said Darlene. She stood up and went to the end of the runway and stood in line behind Jodi, ready to try another vault.

"Boy, she sure landed wrong," I said to Cindi.

"She's right, you know," said Cindi.

"What are you talking about?"

"You aren't trying hard enough," said Cindi. "You always want the rest of us to feel sorry for you because you're just starting up again. But it's hard for the rest of us, too, you know. We're all beginners with Patrick."

"Hey," I said, really beginning to feel a little hurt. "You know the only reason I'm here is because of you. I don't have to be here."

"That's right," said Cindi.

"Hey, wait a minute. When did you start siding with Darlene all the time? I thought you were supposed to be my best friend."

"I *am* your best friend," said Cindi, not sounding it at all. "I just think that Darlene's got a point."

"What happened to that flowing-together-through-life-like-a-river stuff that you wrote to me from camp?"

"Oh, Lauren," said Cindi.

Not exactly the words you wanted to hear from your best friend. I was looking for something more like, "Oh, Lauren, I'm sorry." Or "Oh, Lauren, you're right, and I'm wrong. We have all been picking on you."

Just then Patrick interrupted us. "Girls," he said. "I think you've had enough rest. Come here and do some conditioning."

Cindi jumped up. I saw her whisper something to Darlene. They both looked at me.

I couldn't believe it. All I had done was complain a little bit about a stupid vault, and I felt like I'd lost my best friend. Sometimes I hated gymnastics, just hated it.

8

You Ought to Be in Movies

Patrick said that every gymnast goes through a period where nothing seems to be going right. Welcome to the life-styles of the stuck-in-the-mud.

We had only one week before the competition in front of our parents and the other club members. Instead of getting better I had a feeling I was moving backward.

Patrick told me I was doing fine, that he was pleased with my progress, but I kept feeling I was getting worse and worse.

Then one afternoon when we were working on the beam, my dad suddenly walked in. I couldn't believe it. He wasn't supposed to pick me up.

I went over to him. "What are you doing here?" I asked.

Dad smiled at me. "You were complaining that I'd never seen you work out, never even seen the gym. I decided you were right. I was being stubborn. You say you love it. You shouldn't always have to do what we think. I came to check it out."

I groaned.

"What's wrong?" Dad asked.

"I'm not having a good day," I said.

Dad put his arm around me. "I'm not here to judge you. This place looks great." Cindi waved to him. Darlene gave him a shy smile. Becky turned her camera on us as if she were the inquiring reporter.

"Could you turn this way, Mr. Baca?" she said. "Now, smile, Lauren."

I stuck my tongue out at her.

"Who is she?" Dad whispered to me.

"A pain in the neck," I whispered back.

Patrick stopped what he was doing and came over to us.

"I'm so glad that you stopped by," said Patrick. "I like to have the parents see what we're doing."

I looked up at Patrick, hoping to see that he was kidding, but his blue eyes looked serious. He was using that tone that my teachers use with my mom and dad. It's just a little bit phony.

"Your place is pretty impressive," said Dad. "It brings back lots of memories. When Lauren used to take gymnastics classes we'd go watch her on the board."

"Beam," I said.

"Right," said Dad.

"Well, Lauren's gotten back in the groove quickly," said Patrick.

"Yeah, it's more like a rut," I said.

Patrick ruffled my hair. "You're just going through a rough patch," he said. "She's really very good."

Cindi and Darlene stopped stretching out and came over to us. "Hi, Carl," said Cindi.

Dad put an arm around Cindi. "How's the gymnast?" he asked.

"Great," said Cindi. "We pinecones are putting on a show for you in just a week. Are you coming to watch?"

"I wouldn't miss it," said Dad.

I hated that Dad called Cindi "the gymnast." I was a gymnast, too.

Dad must have caught my look. "Lauren, you want Mom and me to come next week, don't you?" he asked.

"Of course we want you here," boomed Patrick. "Let's show your dad the routine you'll do on the beam."

The beam was one of my better events. Even as a little kid, I've never been afraid of heights.

I can climb trees to the top branch. I can play on top of garage roofs. I feel good on the beam.

Patrick started with Jodi first. Jodi wasn't particularly graceful on the beam, but she was fearless. She did a backward somersault so quickly that she almost fell off, but she didn't try to grab for the beam with her hands.

"Control, control!" shouted Patrick.

Jodi nodded, but she didn't look in control as she kicked up into two 180° turns, and again almost fell off the beam. Yet she saved herself. Her routine ended with a cartwheel from the beam onto the mat.

Patrick spotted her for her dismount, but she really didn't need a spot. She hit it perfectly.

"That was good, Jodi, but you've got to learn to slow it down. You speed through it."

I saw Jodi glance at her mom, who was watching her across the floor. I felt for Jodi. It was hard enough having my dad there for just one day. I knew it wasn't easy for Jodi having her mom around all the time, always watching her when she messed up.

Then Patrick crooked his finger at me. "Your turn, Lauren," he said.

"Are you sure? I think it's Cindi's turn."

Patrick smiled at me. "Come on, we'll show your father what you can do."

I think those were the words that sunk me. My

routine was a lot easier than Jodi's. I only had to do a forward roll, not a backward somersault, and I did it right. My hips didn't wobble off the beam, and Patrick didn't even have to put out a hand to balance me.

I was feeling pretty confident. There are some moments when the beam does feel solid, just like Patrick told us to imagine it during creative rest, like the beam is a solid carpeted floor beneath you. I did a curtsy, and a little scissors leap on the beam. I was going fine.

Then it came time for my dismount. I knew Patrick was there to catch me if I fell. In order to do a cartwheel from the end of the beam, you have to throw yourself in the air.

As Jodi said, it is a proven fact that we are born with a fear of falling.

It is a proven fact that I was born with a fear of failing in front of my dad.

I know Dad didn't want to make me nervous. But I froze.

I stood near the end of the beam in a lunge, my hands over my head, ready to do my cartwheel, and I couldn't move.

"Now," whispered Patrick.

I shook my head, my toes curling around the edges of the beam, something you are not supposed to do.

"I'm right here," whispered Patrick. "Just put

your hands down on the beam and kick it out."

"I can't," I whispered through my teeth.

"Come on, Lauren. Don't think! Do!" Patrick urged.

My front leg shook.

"Is something wrong?" asked Dad, getting up from the bench.

"No," said Patrick. "Lauren can do it. Give her a chance."

I looked down at Patrick. I trusted him. I knew he wouldn't let me hurt myself, but it was as if my feet were welded to the beam.

I might have stayed there forever.

Patrick put his hands on my waist. "Just jump down," he said. "It happens to everybody," he whispered. I refused to move.

"Becky," he shouted. "Come spot her on the other side."

"Becky! Not her," I said.

I saw Becky come toward the beam, still carrying her stupid camera.

I got down on my hands and knees and crawled off the beam.

Patrick looked at me. "Lauren, come back here," he said.

Dad looked a little disturbed.

"Get back up," said Patrick.

My legs were shaking.

"I don't think I can," I said. I was near tears. The rest of the girls were completely silent.

"Look at me," said Patrick.

I looked up at him. I expected him to have a frown on his face. He smiled at me.

"Is this the end of the world?" he asked, patting the end of the beam.

I shook my head.

"It's the end of the beam, isn't it?" he said. "The cartwheel round-off off the beam *is* scary because, in a way, I'm asking you to jump eight feet, but your head and hands will be way down here." He patted the beam. "You've got a great cartwheel on the ground. I wouldn't ask you to do anything you can't do. You know that."

"My head knows it; my body doesn't."

"Get back up there," said Patrick. I jumped back up on the beam.

"Do your routine from the beginning," said Patrick.

I did it, but this time when I did my forward somersault, I almost fell off. Patrick shoveled my hips back onto the beam.

Then it came time for my dismount again.

I lunged, took a deep breath, and then started my cartwheel, diving for the end of the beam, with my hands.

I felt the end of the beam with my fingers, and

I twisted in the air, and the next thing I knew I was on the mat on my butt.

Patrick grinned at me. "That wasn't bad," he said. "You'll try it again later."

I went over to my dad. "Did you see me?" I said proudly. "I did it the second time."

Dad nodded. "Honey, you looked so miserable up there the first time. Nobody's making you come here. Are you sure it's for you?"

I didn't have time to answer. Becky came up to us. She handed me a videocassette. "Here, Lauren," she said. "Maybe you want to watch this with your folks."

"What's this?" I asked.

"Something to help you," said Becky. "I know how much watching my videotapes has helped me. Patrick hopes to get his own video equipment soon, but in the meantime, I help out with mine."

"That's very nice of you," said Dad.

"Lauren is one of my special projects," said Becky. "I just love to watch the little pinecones grow."

I looked down at the videocassette in my hand.

Now, why was I feeling suspicious?

What's Playing?
A Horror Show!

"Becky made a videotape just for you?" Cindi asked me incredulously. Dad was outside waiting to drive me home.

"She gave it to Dad, saying that this was something she thought my whole family would enjoy," I said.

"Knowing her it's probably X-rated," said Darlene.

"I don't think we should let you look at it alone," said Cindi.

We all ended up piled in our car. "That girl who made the videotape seemed like such a nice girl," said Dad. "I want to see that videotape."

"We'll screen it for you, Carl," said Cindi quickly.

I was grateful to her.

When we got to my house, luckily Mom was home, and Dad went into the kitchen to help her with dinner.

I took everybody into the den.

"Why do I have the feeling that this is going to be a horror show?" I asked.

I pushed the play button. There was no sound with the picture. The first picture showed me missing the vault and practically kneeing Patrick in the groin. There I was, running as hard as I could for the springboard and then going up less than one inch.

Then Becky had captured me in slow motion, frozen at the end of the beam, looking like a little kid afraid to dive into a pool.

The tape only lasted about five minutes. Whenever the tape cut away from me, it showed Becky in all her perfection. The message was clear. I was out of my league.

Darlene and Jodi stared at the set, not saying a word.

"She's a creep," said Cindi.

"She said she did it for my own good," I said.

"Yeah, well, if you believe that, you still believe in the tooth fairy."

"I do believe in the tooth fairy," I admitted.

"Why did she go to all that trouble?" Darlene asked.

" 'Cause she wants Lauren to quit," said Cindi.

"Why me? Why not you?" I asked.

Cindi shrugged. "It's a mystery."

"I mean, it's not like I'm a challenge to her or anything," I said. "You guys are all better. I looked like a complete idiot out there. Somehow I didn't know how bad I was."

"You don't usually look so bad," said Darlene.

"Thanks," I mumbled. "That's a great compliment."

"I mean it. Anyone can look bad. You should see the tape my dad has. . . . He collects tapes of all his mistakes."

"What does he do? Hire somebody to follow him around at work?" I asked.

"No, they do that anyhow," said Darlene. She grimaced.

"What does your dad do?" Cindi asked. "I've never met him.

"Neither have I," said Jodi.

I pressed the rewind button. As bad as the tape was, I was sort of fascinated with it. Somehow seeing it the second time around made me laugh.

"My dad does that, too," said Darlene.

"What?" I asked.

"Laugh at himself," said Darlene. "He thinks it's the most important thing an athlete can do."

"An athlete?" I asked.

"Yeah," muttered Darlene. "He's a football player."

"Big Beef!" shrieked Cindi. "That's your dad, isn't it? I never connected it."

"Well, I don't like people to know," said Darlene. "Everybody always makes such a big deal about it, but seeing that tape just reminded me of him. Besides, you'd find out soon enough. He's coming to the competition."

"Wait till my brother hears. He'll definitely come," said Cindi. Then she glanced at Darlene. "Whoops, sorry. I guess that's the attention you meant when you said it bothered you."

"It doesn't bother me when you get excited," said Darlene. "I know you guys aren't my friends just because of him."

"Does he really have a tape of all his mistakes?" I asked.

Darlene nodded. "It's like one of those worst-plays-of-the-month tapes, only it's all of Dad, of him missing blocks, of him trying to tackle someone who isn't there. He says it helps him relax."

"What did you say?" I asked.

"I said it helps him relax."

"No, before that you said that all athletes laugh at themselves."

"Well, not all," said Darlene. "But my dad says that he thinks all athletes need to."

"You called me an athlete," I said proudly.

"Right," said Darlene. "If you weren't an athlete, you wouldn't even be out there trying."

"She's right," said Jodi. "I should know. I come from a family of athletes, too." Jodi giggled.

"What's so funny?" I asked.

"I don't know," she said. "I was just thinking of Mom laughing at a videotape of her mistakes. I can't picture it."

"I like your mom," said Darlene. "She's a great coach."

"I know," said Jodi. "It's just that she takes gymnastics pretty seriously."

"Well, my dad takes football very seriously," said Darlene. "But he does like to laugh."

I flicked on the videotape once more and watched me miss my vault.

"Yeah, well, right now Becky thinks she's got the last laugh."

"You can't quit on us," said Cindi. "Think of the satisfaction it would give Becky."

"I'm not going to quit," I said. "No way. But who do we know who has absolutely *no* sense of humor?"

"Becky!" we all said in unison.

"Anyone without a sense of humor we can beat," I said.

"Do you have a plan?" asked Cindi.

"Just a little reverse psychology of our own," I said. "She tried to out-psych us. We'll out-psych her."

I grinned.

Revenge was sweet.

10

It's No Fun
to Be Hated

The next day when we were starting our warm-ups, I purposely sat down next to Becky. She seemed surprised. "Becky," I said. "I just have to talk to you."

Becky smiled at me. "I guess you watched the videotape," she said.

"It was wonderful!" I exclaimed. "I mean, I can't tell you what it did for me."

"What is that nut talking about?" asked Gloria.

"Becky didn't do one for you?" I asked innocently.

"Do what?" Gloria asked.

"It changed my life," I said. "I mean, I was considering quitting. I felt so bad about how

91

things were going. But Becky went to all that trouble for me. She made me a tape of my mistakes so I could learn from them."

Cindi came up at that moment. We had planned it.

"I saw Lauren's videotape," she said. "It was fantastic. Could you make one for me?"

"Me, too," said Darlene.

"Hey, I'd like one," shouted Charlene, another of the older kids.

"I can't do one for everyone," Becky said.

"Well, that's pretty selfish," said Cindi, with her hands on her hips.

"Yeah," echoed Gloria. "I'm your best friend. But you made one for that little creep."

"She may be little. But she's no creep," said Cindi. "In fact, watching that film made me realize how good Lauren is."

"Huh?" said Becky.

"That's right," said Darlene. "The videotape showed all of Lauren's mistakes, but even making a mistake, she showed good form."

The warm-ups had practically stopped as everyone sat in a circle around Becky, all of them wanting their very own videotape before the competition next week.

"What's going on?" asked Patrick. "I don't remember calling for a gossip circle."

"It's creative talk," I said, grabbing my toes and stretching out.

"Patrick," Gloria whined, "it's not fair. Becky's helping Lauren, but she won't help the rest of us."

Patrick reared his head back, looking skeptical. He studied me. Patrick wasn't dumb. I knew he realized that Becky wasn't exactly my best friend.

"What did Becky do for Lauren?" he asked.

"She made a videotape of Lauren, but she won't make one of the rest of us," said Gloria.

"It sure surprised me," I said, putting on my most innocent voice. "It's great, Patrick. I really learned from it."

"Let me see it," said Patrick. I went in the locker room and brought out the videotape. Patrick had a TV and a VCR near the couches where the parents wait for us.

He put my tape into the machine.

Cindi took my hand. Our plan wouldn't work if I got embarrassed.

Darlene winked at me.

Then, just as the tape started to play, Darlene, Cindi, Jodi and I stood up and took out kazoos we had hidden behind our backs. We blared out the fanfare trumpet theme for the Olympics.

"Up close and personal with Lauren Baca," said

93

Jodi. "Lauren Baca is with us now, ready to share with you her own impressions of her triumph at the Evergreen Gymastics Academy."

"Thank you so much," I simpered.

The tape showed me falling off the vault onto my head. "I owe everything to the fact that my coach dropped me on the head so many times when I was just starting out," I said.

Patrick guffawed.

Then Darlene took center stage. "Now we show the great Lauren Baca in her triumph on the beam."

The tape showed me frozen in fear on the beam. "Yes, Darlene," I said into the imaginary microphone she held up to my mouth, "I'm so glad you showed this to our listening audience. This was an exercise invented by my great coach, Patrick Harmon. 'Anyone can do a round-off dismount,' Coach Harmon used to say. 'But *how long* can one person stay on the beam?' I used to practice this move, or rather this *un*-move, for hours on the beam."

The tape showed Patrick urging me to move. "You see the patient look on Coach Harmon's face as he encourages me to stand there as long as I want."

Patrick was holding his sides, he was laughing so hard. The other girls were rolling on the floor.

Becky's cheeks were bright red.

94

The tape went blank. Darlene kept her hand up to my mouth.

"Do you have anything else you'd like to say?"

"Yes, I owe it all to Becky Dyson. When I was just a little pinecone, lying on the cold, cold ground, she encouraged me to be the best nut I could be."

"And how did she do that?" Darlene asked.

"She taught me to be strong," I said. I glanced at Becky. I wasn't exactly kidding.

Patrick stood up. "That was great, Becky," he said. "It's a great tool. If your parents wouldn't mind, maybe you could make one for the other girls, too."

"But that's a lot of work," complained Becky.

Patrick nodded. "But it will be so worthwhile," he said. "I'd like you to share your good sportsmanship with all the girls, not just Lauren."

Becky glared at me.

"Thank you, Becky, so much," I said, bowing from the waist. I put my arm around her shoulder as if she were my best friend.

She shook my hand off. "That was not funny," she said.

"I thought it was," I said.

"I don't want to make videotapes for everybody. It'll be a pain."

"Well, I'm just giving you a chance to show everyone what a good sport you are," I said.

95

"I'll get you back," Becky hissed at me. I mean *actually* hissed.

"Hey," I shouted after her. "Don't lose your sense of humor!"

"What was that all about?" Cindi and Darlene asked.

"She's really mad," I said.

"Well, of course," said Darlene. "We made her look like a fool. We were terrific. It went great. We got her right in the funny bone."

"I know," I said. "But she sounded like she really hates me."

"Don't worry about it," said Cindi.

I'd never had anyone hate me before. It had been easy to make fun of Becky, and it had been hilarious, and she deserved it.

But let me tell you, I didn't like being hated.

Besides, I still hadn't solved the real mystery. Why had she singled me out in the first place?

11

It's Not
That Funny!

"Way to go, Lauren," shouted Patrick. I had missed my landing on the vault and fallen flat on my back, but Patrick was cheering like I had just made a touchdown.

"What are you cheering about? I fell on my landing."

Sarah grinned at me. "Don't worry about your landing," she said. "You did it. Get in line and try it again." Sarah and Patrick were spotting us on either side of the vault.

I picked myself up and walked to the beginning of the line as Becky took off for her vault. We were practicing the "handstand" vaults. We had to jump off the springboard into a handstand on the vault and then flip over onto the landing mat.

It looks really hard, much harder than the squat mount that had been giving me so much trouble, but I actually found it easier. Maybe it's because I love doing handstands, but I was feeling good.

Becky nailed her vault. Patrick nodded at her. "Good one," he said. "But remember, keep your arms stiff when you hit the vault. Your elbows were bent."

Becky looked annoyed.

She followed me back down the runway to get in line.

"Good vault," I said.

She shrugged. We watched Darlene race down the runway. Darlene mistimed her jump on the board and Patrick had to push her into the handstand. He and Darlene laughed at her mistake. It was our last day to practice before our parents were coming to watch the pinecones perform. Patrick kept telling us not to be nervous, but of course that only made us more nervous. He kept saying that we wouldn't be competing against strangers, just against each other. That also made me nervous.

Becky really hadn't spoken to me since we had made fun of her. Every time she saw me she glared at me, and that was making me nervous.

Do you get the idea that I was nervous?

Jodi was standing in line behind me. I was glad that she was between me and Becky.

Becky whispered something into Jodi's ear. Jodi said something I couldn't catch.

Then Becky whispered something back and giggled.

Jodi blushed.

Becky ran into the corner and whispered something to Gloria. They both looked at me.

"What did she say to you?" I asked Jodi.

"Nothing," said Jodi.

"It was something," I said. "You blushed."

"She just doesn't like you," said Jodi. "Don't let it bother you."

"Don't let it bother me? What did she say?"

"She made a dumb joke," said Jodi. "She asked me what kind of nut you reminded me of."

"So?"

"I said, we're all pinecones. . . ."

"And. . . ." I knew an insult was coming.

"She said you reminded her of a *dough*nut."

I pulled my stomach in. "We all can't be skinny."

"You're not fat. You're muscular," said Jodi. "Don't let her get to you. Having an enemy like her is a compliment."

"Yeah, but she's not cracking jokes about you," I said.

It was time for my vault. Naturally, I messed up.

I could hear Becky giggling way across the room. Cindi told me to ignore Becky. Jodi said that having Becky as an enemy was a compliment to my good taste. But Becky didn't hate Jodi. She didn't hate Cindi. She hated me. Why me? I had to know.

At the end of class, in the locker room, I went up to Becky again.

"Can I talk to you?" I asked.

"What do you want?" Becky demanded. She rolled up her leotard and stuffed it in her gym bag.

"I'm curious," I said.

Becky looked at me suspiciously.

"Curious about what?" she asked.

"Why me?" I asked.

"I give," said Becky. "Why you? Is this a riddle?"

"Yeah, like your riddle calling me a 'doughnut.' That was mean. No, I meant it seriously. Why did you make that tape for me?"

"You don't get it, do you?" asked Becky. She slung her gym bag over her shoulder.

"Don't get what? Come on, Becky. Why did you go to all that trouble?"

Becky turned around. She put down her gym bag and stared at me, her weight on one leg, her hand on her hip.

She made me feel about two years old. "I wanted you to quit," she said finally.

"Quit? Me?"

"Quit? Me?" she echoed in a mocking voice.

I just didn't get it. "Why should I bother you?" I asked. "You never met me before I came here, and I'm the worst of the new kids. If you'd want anyone to quit, I'd think it'd be Jodi or Darlene or Cindi, not me."

Becky looked at me in disgust. "Yeah, and that's why Patrick spends so much time with you, isn't it?"

"Yes, 'cause I need it."

Becky took a step closer to me. "Are you trying another mind game on me?" she asked.

"No," I protested.

"Then you're dumber than I thought," she said. She started to leave.

I grabbed the strap of her gym bag. "Becky, you can't say that. I'm not dumb, but I really don't understand. Why do you hate me?"

" 'Cause you're good, dumbo," said Becky. "And Patrick likes you. I don't like coaches' pets. They're not good for the team."

"But I haven't even made the team."

Becky pulled on the strap of her gym bag. Her face was inches from mine.

"You really think I'm good?" I asked.

Becky nodded, her face serious.

"You were worried about me?" I exclaimed. I was still convinced that this was some sort of trick that Becky was playing on me.

101

"I didn't like it that Patrick was paying so much attention to you," she said.

"Patrick helps me because I have such a hard time getting everything."

"You should stop thinking of yourself as the beginner," said Becky.

I smiled at her. "You know, that's what my friends said."

"Yeah, well, I'm sure you don't consider *me* a friend," Becky said.

"Well, not exactly. I thought you hated me."

Becky stuck her hand out. I shook it, a little confused. "It looks like you're going to stick around," she said. "We might as well be friends. You know, my mom always says that if you can't fight them, join them."

"I thought it was 'if you can't beat them, join them,' " I said.

"Whatever," said Becky. "But since we're gonna be around each other a lot, it's stupid to hate each other."

"Great," I said, relieved. "I really don't like having enemies."

"Me, neither," said Becky. "Oh, by the way," she said. "I've got a hint for you on the vault."

"Yeah?"

"Just as you're going into your handstand, bend your elbow a little. It'll give you power."

"But that's the exact opposite of what Patrick's been saying."

"I know," said Becky. "But you saw my vault, didn't you? It was great. I mean, Patrick's a terrific coach, but I've taken lessons all over. I had a coach whose specialty was the vault. She taught me that if you bend your elbow just a tad, it acts like a piston getting you over. Understand?"

I shook my head. "Uh, not exactly."

"See, if you don't bend your arms, you've got nothing to push you up and over. Get it?"

I didn't want to admit that I didn't know a piston from a pistol. But what she was saying sort of made sense.

"I'll try it," I said.

I looked up and noticed that Cindi, Darlene, and Jodi were in the corner looking at us.

"Come on," I said to Becky. "Come on over to the other pinecones. They're not so bad, either."

"I don't have time," said Becky. "I'll see you guys tomorrow."

She waved at Cindi, Darlene, and Jodi and left the locker room.

"What were you talking to *her* for?" Cindi demanded after she left.

"She's okay," I said. "You know, I've been feeling bad. I really didn't understand why she was picking on me, so I asked her."

"And what did she say?" Darlene asked suspiciously.

I giggled. "She was jealous," I said. "She thought I was good."

Cindi started laughing so hard she couldn't stop.

"It's not *that* funny," I said.

12

This Time, Don't Scare Us to Death

"Gymnastics causes more stress than any other sport. It's a proven fact," I said as I pulled on my official Evergreen leotard.

The other kids in the locker room groaned. "It's true," I said. "I saw a chart about what causes stress in kids. Gymnastics was way up there. The only thing that causes more stress is giving a band solo or being in a wrestling match."

"Where does she get these facts?" Jodi asked.

"It's a proven fact," said Cindi, "that sick facts seek Lauren out."

"I saw it in a book that Patrick has," I said. "Basketball doesn't cause as much stress, and even taking a test isn't as bad. It's because gymnastics is an individual sport. We're all alone out there. I think I'd rather be playing a band solo."

"You don't play an instrument. You're tone-deaf," Cindi reminded me. "Remember, in kindergarten, when the teacher asked you to play the erasers?"

"The erasers?" asked Darlene.

"Yeah," I admitted. "It wasn't until third grade that I realized she wanted me to play something that didn't make any noise."

"Forget the erasers," said Darlene. "We're a team. We're the Pinecones."

"But we're competing against each other," I argued. "And I think I may get sick."

"Please," pleaded Jodi. "Don't talk about being sick. I've already thrown up this morning."

"You? You're going to be great," I said. It was hard to think of Jodi being nervous.

"I always throw up before a competition," said Jodi. "It's a tradition with me."

"After you've been sick, how do you do?" asked Cindi.

Jodi grinned. "Sometimes great," she admitted.

"Maybe I should go throw up," I said.

"Please, no," said Cindi. "It might be catching. Personally I don't want to throw up, even if it's a proven fact that I'd do better afterward."

"It's not," said Jodi. "It doesn't work for everybody."

"You know what I'm worried about?" I said. "That I'm going to get chalk all over my leotard."

"You guys are driving me crazy," said Darlene. "Will you stop it? You're making me worried."

"What is this, the worry club?" asked Becky when she came in to get us. "Are you ready?"

She looked me up and down. "Do you want me to videotape your performance?" she asked.

I shook my head. "No thanks, we've got our own video crew out there."

Becky looked confused.

"It's my Dad," said Darlene sweetly. "He's videotaping all of us. But thanks, Becky. You're a peach."

Becky walked beside me. "Remember that advice I gave you for the vault," she whispered.

Then she left us. She was to lead the parade of gymnasts.

"What did she want?" Cindi asked.

"You know, she's really not so bad," I said.

Darlene held her fingers to her nose. "I think you've gotten too close."

"Come on, Darlene. I mean it. Maybe we've humiliated her enough. I swear, Becky really isn't as bad as we thought," I said.

Becky stuck her head back into the locker room. "Will you kids hurry up?" she said. "Patrick's getting mad."

I sighed. "Okay . . . look, we can't let anything

shake our concentration. Let's just go out there and pray we don't screw up. We're gonna be great. Think creative rest."

I grabbed Cindi as we were going through the door. "Good luck," I said.

Cindi nodded, but she didn't smile.

"You're not mad at me, are you?" I asked.

"Maybe Becky's your best new friend," she said.

"She's not," I protested. "I just think we may have misjudged her."

Cindi raised her eyebrows. "I think she's smooth and very dangerous," she said.

"Like shark-infested custard?"

Cindi laughed. "Come on, we've got more than Becky to worry about. First we've got to get through our routines."

We walked out into the gym and suddenly heard the applause. It seemed to echo from the sky-lights. I mean, there really weren't that many people there, but Cindi's brothers could make a lot of noise. They were all whistling and holler-ing. So was my grandmother. My parents were applauding politely.

All the guests were sitting on folding chairs. It was very easy to pick out Darlene's dad. He practically needed two seats. He was the big-gest — not fat — but just the biggest man I had ever seen.

My parents were sitting in the front row. They

were clapping and grinning. That's when I really started to get nervous.

Patrick clapped his hands once and stood in front of all the parents. "I'd like to welcome you all to the first meet with my promising Pinecones. And I want to say that this group of newcomers is one of the best I've had in a long time."

"I bet he says that to all the groups," whispered Cindi.

But Patrick continued. "I don't mean that they're the best gymnasts . . . ," he paused.

"I bet he doesn't say *that* to all the groups," I whispered.

"These girls stand out because of the way they work together," said Patrick. "And I'd rather have kids who get along than perfect tens."

"Why not have both?" I shouted.

Patrick laughed. "As you can see, we haven't struck fear into the hearts of these girls, yet. Lauren, if I take you into real competition, no shouting at the judges."

My father laughed, but he looked a little uncomfortable.

Patrick introduced the judges. They were two gymnastics coaches from a school in downtown Denver who were friends of his. I saw them take out their clipboards and then it really hit me. My mouth went dry.

Patrick had let us pick our own music for our

floor routine. We were doing it to an old Bob Marley reggae tune, "Get Up, Stand Up." In real competition we wouldn't be able to use music with words, but somehow the song, "Get Up, Stand Up" seemed very appropriate. Cindi had picked the music.

One consequence of being the newest was that I got to go first in all the events. In a way I was glad, glad to get them over with. Our floor exercise started with a forward walkover and a one-armed cartwheel. I did the first two moves perfectly, but I needed Patrick's help spotting me on a roundoff into a back flip. But that was okay. He whispered "great" to me, and I kept going just like he had told me to do if I made a mistake.

I landed on the floor in a graceful torso swing. I couldn't believe it. I had done it!

Darlene, Jodi, and everyone clapped loudly for me. I discovered something in that moment. I was a ham. I loved the applause. I couldn't wait for my next event.

The judges' scores came up. I got a 4.8 out of ten. I thought that was terrible. But Cindi only got a 5.1 and Jodi got the highest, and hers was only a 6.3.

Jodi went through her routine on the uneven bars incredibly fast. "Slow down, slow down," I heard her mom whisper.

Jodi just moved faster and faster, but she almost finished her routine without a single mistake. She was by far the best of the four of us. Then on her last move from the high bar to the low bar, her momentum was just too much. Even I could tell she was going too fast. She hit the low bar with a thud. She managed to save the routine by bending her leg and regrasping the bar, but it cost her two tenths of a point just for having to move her hands. The bent legs cost her three tenths of a point.

Darlene did exceptionally well on the uneven bars. She was much more daring than we had ever seen her in practice, and the judges scored her just a tenth of a point ahead of Jodi. I was glad that I didn't fall off, and I got a 4.6.

Then it was time for the balance beam.

Patrick stood at the side of the beam in case any of us needed a spot. In a real competition, he wouldn't be there.

I had to keep cool so I wouldn't fall. I remembered Patrick telling me to "concentrate," to complete one whole move without worrying about the next. I went through my routine, and it was almost over.

But then it was time for my roundoff dismount. I looked up from the beam and saw Becky watching me. I wondered if she thought I'd freeze the way I had before.

"You can do it," Patrick whispered.

He held out a hand to let me know he was there. But I ignored his hand and lunged. Then I kicked my legs out from under me and I was in a cartwheel. I was up in the air and then down. I turned to round off towards the beam, stretching out my toes like Patrick had taught me and bending my legs. I brought my arms up over my head, and I didn't fall down.

Patrick clapped his hands and grinned at me.

"You're a trouper, Lauren!" he said. "You don't quit."

I waved to my mom and dad, who were applauding and looking very proud of me.

"Thanks, Patrick," I said. "I never quit."

Then it was time for our vaults.

Cindi went first. "Good luck," I whispered. She nodded, her face a blank. But that was the look Cindi always had when she concentrated.

She shook her arms and legs like a swimmer about to dive into the pool. She blew her hair off her forehead and jogged in place.

Patrick stood at the end of the eight-foot runway ready to give her help if she needed it.

She squared her shoulders and narrowed her eyes.

She raised her arm and exploded down the runway, hitting the springboard at the end like a jackhammer. She flew up in the air and then launched into a handstand over the vault. As she was coming down, she stretched out her toes and legs so she landed way down on the crash mat, and she kept her balance!

"All right!" I shouted as Cindi shot her arms up in victory. She turned towards the audience, a big grin dancing across her face.

Cindi waited for her score. She got a 6.8, her highest score on any event.

"You can do it, too," I heard a voice whisper to me. It was Becky. I started to rub my hands, which still had chalk on them from my routine on the uneven bars.

"Don't rub the chalk off," warned Becky. "It'll help you on the vault. And remember what I told you. Just as you go into your handstand, bend your elbows."

"Okay, thanks," I whispered.

I stood at the end of the runway. I raised my right hand. I ran as fast as I could. If ever I needed that explosive power, it was now.

I jumped on the springboard with both feet and I was soaring. I dove for the vault with my hands and bent my elbows, then I slipped off, like an out-of-control watermelon seed. I didn't know where I was.

I landed flat on my back. I couldn't breathe.

Patrick was standing over me, lifting my rib

cage. Mom and Dad must have set a speed record themselves for getting out of a chair and across the room.

"Is she okay? Lauren!" cried Mom.

It is very hard to talk when you've had all the air knocked out of you.

I tried to nod.

"Lauren. Move your arms and legs," Patrick ordered. I could do that. I just couldn't talk. I waved my arms and legs like an octopus bath toy whose mainspring wasn't working very well.

Patrick's face looked relieved. "She's okay!" he said to my parents.

I tried to sit up. "Take it easy," said Patrick. "Catch your breath. You don't have to do your second vault."

"I want to," I gasped. "Just give me a second."

Mom and Dad looked worried. Then Mom bent down and gripped my shoulder. "Do it again," she whispered. "You've got a second chance."

"Good luck," Dad whispered. "This time, don't scare us to death."

Patrick held out his hand and helped me to my feet. I looked back at the vault. It looked huge to me.

Patrick was staring down at his hand. "You had chalk dust on your palm," he said.

"Yeah, I know. I left it on after the uneven bars. I thought it would help."

Patrick looked furious. "No wonder you nearly killed yourself!" he said. "There's no way you could have made that vault if your hands were slippery."

"But . . . but. . . ."

I looked down the runway at Becky who was whispering in Gloria's ear.

"Go rest and think about your next vault," said Patrick. "It's time for Cindi's second vault."

I sat on a bench and watched Cindi complete her second vault. It was as great as her first.

She came and sat down next to me. "You okay?" she asked.

"Yeah. You were fantastic!"

"You gonna do your second vault?" Cindi asked.

I didn't answer right away. I stood up. "Tell me," I asked. "When you do your handstand on the vault, do you bend your arms?"

"Are you kidding?" said Cindi. "The only thing that gets you over is if you keep your arms straight."

"I thought so," I said.

I shook my shoulders. "You don't have to do your second vault, you know," said Cindi.

"Oh, yes, I do," I said.

13

The Best Revenge

I stood at the edge of the mat. Everyone was waiting for me to do my second vault, but I wasn't ready. My shoulder hurt where I had landed on it.

I saw Patrick at the end of the runway, right next to the vault. I knew that he'd spot me *if* I needed it, but if he touched me my vault wouldn't count.

I thought about everything he had taught me about handstands.

I glanced around. Becky was biting her fingernails. Good. I liked that she was nervous. Mom gave me a small smile. Dad nodded at me, just a slight smile on his lips. He looked proud of me.

Then I raised my right hand to show the judges

I was ready. I ran. I ran like that very first day when I had beaten Cindi. I ran fast, but this time there was no one I was trying to beat. I was running for myself.

I hit the board, standing tall, and I reached out for the vault with my hands. As soon as my hands touched the vault, I straightened my elbows as stiff as I could, pushing down on the vault hard into my handstand.

I flipped over and stretched my legs, reaching for the mat. At touchdown I leaned backward, bending my hips as if I were sitting down. I kept my balance. I didn't fall backward.

I threw my arms over my head.

Then I turned. Patrick crushed me in a bear hug.

"You did it!"

He held on to me while we waited for the judges' scores. 6.9. I had beat Cindi's score!

"You bet I did it!" I shouted.

I ran back along the runway.

Becky stood on one side. She looked like she was afraid I was going to hit her.

I didn't.

I stuck my tongue out at her.

Then I jumped into the arms of Cindi, Darlene, and Jodi, who were standing and cheering for me.

"That was some vault!" exclaimed Cindi.

I grinned.

Patrick came to our group. He put his arm around us. "You girls were terrific," he said.

He held his hand up. "That concludes our exhibition of my little Pinecones," he said. "And I think you've got some idea of the range of these girls. The overall winner, a terrific competitor, is Cindi Jockett. Cindi is proof that consistency counts."

I gave Cindi a hug. She deserved it. She hadn't won any of the four events, but she had come in close to the winner in all four.

But the rest of us each had something to be proud of, too. Darlene had won on the beam, and the uneven bars. Jodi had won on the floor exercise, and me, Lauren Baca, *not* the beginner, I had won the vault.

"Now some of the girls who have been with us longer will put on an exhibition," said Patrick. "But before they do, I want to announce that I plan on using all four of the Pinecones on my team when we start competing against other clubs."

"All right!" I exclaimed.

Darlene, Jodi, Cindi, and I all slapped our hands together in the air.

I turned around. Mom and Dad were smiling at me. Dad looked shy and then he gave me a thumbs-up signal. I think my dad secretly liked that I was an athlete. I had a feeling that he'd be at a lot of our meets.

"Now, if my Pinecones will sit down, I'd like the others to get ready," said Patrick.

Becky's mother came up close with her video camera to record every moment of Becky's performance.

I went up to Becky while her mother had the camera on her. Becky kind of flinched as if she didn't know what I was going to do. I waved into the camera. "I just want it to go on record how very much I'm looking forward to competing on Becky Dyson's team," I said. "In fact, I'm looking so forward to it that I'm going to work hard and someday beat her in the individual events, particularly in the vault."

Becky's mother looked confused. "Who *is* this girl?" she asked Becky.

"I'm the competition," I said proudly.

I went to the chalk bin and dipped my hands in the chalk. "What are you doing?" Becky asked me, her voice a little frightened.

I smiled at her. "Your first event is the vault, isn't it?" I whispered, grinning into the camera.

Becky nodded.

"Do you think some chalk dust would help?" I asked Becky. "After all, that's the advice you gave me."

"Uh, no," said Becky quickly.

"Well, good luck!" I said. I gave Becky a friendly pat on the behind, the way all those football players do.

Becky turned to go to the runway for the vault.

My handprint was clearly outlined on her green leotard.

Cindi started to giggle. She pointed out my handprint to Darlene, who nudged Jodi and pointed. I sat down next to them.

Becky looked behind her. She couldn't figure out why people were giggling. My handprint was too far down for her to see.

Her mother rushed forward to try to brush off her leotard, but Becky had already raised her right arm, indicating she was ready to take off for her vault.

She ran. My handprint was like a jogging bull's-eye. The audience started to titter.

I watched Becky.

She didn't let the audience distract her. I'll say one thing for her: she really was a competitor.

She hit the springboard and kept her elbows stiff as she did her handstand on the vault.

She almost nailed her landing, but then she leaned back too far and fell, right on my handprint.

She looked around for the judge's score. 6.3.

Cindi held out her hand. I slapped it. Then I

caught Becky glaring at us, as her mother ran up to her and wiped off her leotard.

Somehow her glares didn't bother me.

I knew Becky was good. She and I would be competing with and against each other in lots of meets.

She couldn't hurt me. Not if I tried my hardest.

Do you want revenge? Get yourself some good friends and go for it. That's my advice.

Going for it is the best revenge of all.

At the end of the exhibition, Patrick asked his four Pinecones to come back out on the mats.

We grabbed hands and ran into the middle of the gym. We weren't just four competitors who happened to be friends. We were a team.

About the Author

Elizabeth Levy decided that the only way she could write about gymnastics was to try it herself. Besides taking classes she is involved with a group of young gymnasts near her home in New York City, and enjoys following their progress.

Elizabeth Levy's other Apple Paperbacks are *A Different Twist, The Computer That Said Steal Me,* and all the other books in THE GYMNASTS series.

She likes visiting schools to give talks and meet her readers. Kids love her presentation's opening. Why? "I start with a cartwheel!" says Levy. "At least I try to."